An Anxiety/Outcast Press Anthology

I0623078

Elegies
in the
dust

ISBN: 978-1-960882-11-0

Front cover image/interior design by:

ANXIETY DRIVEN GRAPHICS

Anxiety / Outcast

contents

Fiction

Poetry

Poetry

Elegies in the dust

WHAT TRAUMA DOES AND WHAT LITERATURE CAN DO

Cassie Premo Steele

Cassie Premo Steele is an environmental poet, novelist, and essayist whose writing focuses on the themes of trauma, healing, creativity, and mindfulness. She holds a Ph.D. in Comparative Literature and Women's, Gender and Sexuality Studies from Emory University in Atlanta, Georgia. She is the author of 18 books, including the groundbreaking scholarly study, We Heal from Memory: Sexton, Lorde, Anzaldúa and The Poetry of Witness, as well as 3 novels and 7 books of poetry, and her poetry has been nominated 7 times for the Pushcart Prize. She was a finalist for the Rita Dove Poetry Award judged by the former US Poet Laureate Joy Harjo. She has also been awarded The DuBose and Dorothy Heyward Society Prize, the Stephanie Ellen Siler Memorial Prize, the John Edward Johnson Prize, the Carrie McCray Literary Award for Poetry, and the Archibald Rutledge Prize named after the first Poet Laureate of South Carolina, where she lives with her wife. Her latest book is the novel, Beaver Girl, published as a collaboration between Anxiety and Outcast Presses.

Trauma is about skipping.

When I was child and danced too hard while a record was playing in our rural Minnesota family room, sometimes the needle would slip, and part of the song would get missed.

This is how trauma works.

We are faced with something that threatens us, and we skip the experience in order to survive it.

It's important to pause here to emphasize that it doesn't matter what caused the skipping. This means that sexual assault, combat, slavery, colonization, interpersonal violence, systemic racism, genocide, and pandemic are all traumatic—not because of the level of threat or fear or violence associated with them, but because of the way we survive them by skipping.

There are over half a million children skipping in Gaza right now.

Skipping means we skip over the feelings. We skip over the story. The mind does not register either the feelings or the story as a way of protecting the survivor and keeping her alive.

So later, when survivors are numb and do not have a story for what happened, this is precisely the evidence that shows that a traumatic experience has occurred.

One day, a UN worker will ask a child, "What happened?"

And the child will not be able to speak.

There is a way to slip this noose, however, and it lies in poetry. Poetry allows us to begin to witness a trauma: It provides the ingredients of feelings without the need for a story, and once we begin to access feeling, we can begin healing.

Somewhere, sometime out of time, a Palestinian child will be given a piece of paper and will write it down. The bombs like black birds falling out of the sky. The food drops like birthday balloons gone awry.

All kinds of stress, not just traumatic ones, can create a fight-flight-freeze response in the amygdala, that small walnut part of the brain at the base of our skull that is primed to keep us alive.

Some call it the lizard brain.

It's the oldest part of us, that primitive and extremely complex (these, interestingly, often go hand-in-hand in the languages of biology and culture) part of our bodies that helps regulate the nervous system.

And the nervous system, in turn, regulates everything: heartbeat, blood pressure, digestion, breathing.

Holding her breath as the sound of a bomb takes its time coming down.

Trauma happens when the amygdala takes over and shuts down the neo-frontal cortex of our brains, that most developed part of us that allows thinking and planning to take place.

It is important to remember that it is not *what* creates a traumatic experience but a *how.*

This is essential for opening a doorway to compassion. There is no trauma Olympics. No gold medals for pain. The shutting down of critical thinking, the intense focus on the present to the exclusion of planning, the fight-flight-freeze response, and the inability to say in a narrative way what happened: These affect everyone equally. The sexual assault survivor and the combat veteran. The accident victim and the Palestinian child.

The generations whose ancestors lived and are living through colonization, removal, genocide, slavery, and economic and environmental disaster.

That boy stealing bread to feed his sister in Rafah is you, pouring another drink.

The first thing we can do in the face of stress or trauma is to get calm.

This is easy to say and much, much harder to do, especially if we haven't received training in childhood or even adulthood in how to do this—and if we live in a culture that encourages the ramping up of fear and anxiety through constant news cycles, social media trends, and alerts and notifications about disasters.

And we all live in that world.

We can learn though, to use the tools of mindfulness to get calm. Focusing on the five senses without judging or labeling, following the breath as it moves in and out, paying attention to the body in a loving way through a body scan, and journaling. These have been proven by numerous studies to be effective at calming the nervous system and allowing us to get grounded.

But we must also feel.

What fight, flight and freeze has in common—and the reason why they are so destructive to our mind-body-spirits in the present and the cascade effect they create that sets up aftereffects in the future—is that there is an absence of feeling while they are happening.

False witnessing happens when stories are told in the media about traumatic events, but the standards of journalism dictate that one omits any true emotional connection that enables people to feel anything but a rubbernecking there-but-for-the-grace-go-I response.

One day, the girl with her bird bomb poem will be interviewed and used on CNN.

The hardest thing about being a survivor is that you never really want to admit how helpless you were.

By claiming even the tiniest thread of agency in a situation, we can tell ourselves that somehow we chose it or could have done something differently—and therefore, it wasn't as bad as it could have been because maybe, just maybe, things could have been worse, and maybe, in the case that something like that happens again, we will know what to do, we can handle it better, and we can maintain a kind of hope, a kind of sense of control, over what was, really was, hopelessly out of control.

In short, survivors blame themselves because that's easier that admitting they had absolutely no control.

Or survivors blame everyone else because that's easier than admitting the pain they carry.

Who will be bombed 76 years from now?

There is a kind of either/or thinking that results from trauma and pretends to be a way of keeping anxiety at bay.

Either/or thinking can be found hiding in words like "always" and "never" and "will" and "won't" and "do" and "don't" and "all" and "nothing."

The word "essay" comes from the French verb *éssayer*, which means "to try."

The children try to leave. The children try to cross the border. The children try to find shelter.

I have tried all my life.

In the second grade, I wrote myself a little note with the capital letters **TRY** and I put it inside my wooden desk— not the kind with the lid that lifted but the more modern one with an open drawer in the front.

This way, every time I went to look for a pencil, or get out my cursive workbook, and especially when it was time for the math textbook, I would remember to **TRY**.

I really didn't need the reminder, though.

I had been striving, pushing, trying all my life.

When I wrote above that I had been "trying all my life," that was a tell.
All my life? Really?

But by second grade, in Mrs. Wolf's classroom, I was already trying to try. I had already written a narrative in my mind about myself as a tryer.

I was already a survivor.

Did surviving make me smart? Or was I born smart, and that's why I survived?

Or is the cause-and-effect construction of these questions connected to the binary thinking of trauma and of Western culture itself?

In any case, I was a really smart little kid. My parents decided I didn't need to go to kindergarten but could start at five years old by going directly into the first grade. I made it through a few months, and then the math got hard.

I was sent back to kindergarten.

Sitting on the floor of the classroom one day with other children who seemed like babies to me now that I had known life on the other side with desks and actual homework, the teacher asked us if we had any suggestions for decorating the classroom for open house night when the parents would come visit.

My hand shot up.

"Yes, Cassie?" she said. She was probably tired of me, this smarty-pants first-grade reject, who always raised her hand first.
"What if we take construction paper, blue and white," I began, visualizing my idea as I spoke and looking around the room. "And cut the white paper into the shape of a fence and put it all around the walls of the room?"

I paused. She nodded almost imperceptibly, mostly so I would finish.

"And then what if we lay blue construction paper all over the floor?"

She scrunched her eyebrows at me. She clearly did not share my vision.

"Watergate," I said. "We could turn the classroom into Watergate. That's what the parents really care about. That's all they talk about."

She breathed a sigh of relief that I was finished, shook her head, and asked, "Any other ideas, children?"

I have another memory about Watergate, and while the first one shows me as clever and precocious, this one makes me quite an unreliable narrator.

My sister and I were in the car. Our mom was driving. Our dad was riding shotgun. And we were in the back seat. They were going to drop us off at school, but, on the way, we were going to get donuts.

The radio was on.

As we pulled into the donut shop parking lot, the president came on and said he was not going to be the president anymore.

My parents were frozen.

The world outside, in a Minnesota winter, was frozen, too. There were banks of snow along the edge of the parking lot. My kindergarten Watergate had become a second-grade Snowalot.

We all listened.

Time slowed.

I could feel that this was very important. I couldn't even tell if my parents were breathing, so still, they were.

I was hungry. I had really been looking forward to that donut. Maybe two. French éclairs were my favorite.

And despite the slowing of time inside the car, the clock was ticking in the outside world, and I was afraid of being late to school.

The memory ends there.

I can't remember if we got donuts, or if we made it to school on time, or anything my parents said.

But I had learned the lesson of the day: People fail.

People fail and they admit it.

The most important person in the country had done something very bad, and he had lied about it, and he got caught, and he could not be the president anymore.

But he had admitted it.

What world leader will admit to the mistakes they are making today against the children of Palestine?

So, from an early age, my parents, simply by following politics, had taught me that knowledge was important, but so was truth, and there were consequences for neglecting either one.

And this is the thing that makes no sense: When I go back to find the date of Nixon's resignation speech, it takes place on the evening of August 8, 1974.

Evening. Not morning before school with donuts.

August. Not snow in the parking lot.

Could they have been listening to the coverage on the radio the morning after, and could there have been a freak August snowstorm overnight?

I go to the Winona, Minnesota, newspaper for that day, and no, the low temperature for that day was in the 50s and high in the 80s with showers and thunderstorms possible.
And while searching for that information, I come across this: "A White House spokesman said the switchboard was so overloaded with calls 'heavily weighted toward expressions of belief in the President' that corps of volunteers had to be assigned to help answer them."

This is not something we clearly remember these days. Perhaps this is like the snow in my memory.

Either the snow was there, or my memory is faulty.

And if we rely on memory for knowledge, and memory fails us, then, according to Socrates, we veer into the realm of evil.

What are we already not remembering about what is happening in Gaza with the weapons our English-speaking nations are paying for?

It takes a long time, and a lot of work, to come to see a traumatic past in a beautiful light.

Literature—everything from the journal entries you write in the middle of the night, to poetry and short stories and fiction—can help us do this.

At first, this seems like a sacrilege—to honor the sacredness of past pain, we must shine a laser beam of sharpness upon it, something that can open and burn the wound, to keep it from clotting over in forgetting and leading to further infection.

The children of Gaza will have to rip open their wounds one day.

Or leave it for their great grandchildren to try to do so with words they cannot say.

That work of healing is what takes a long time and a lot of work. It cannot be rushed. There must not be a surgery scheduled in twenty minutes that might make us do sloppy work on the incision or the sewing of stitches at the end of the operation.

This is the work of writers.

We avoid this. We put it off. We busy ourselves with achievement or work or sports or cleaning the house or going to meetings.

We avoid this by drinking and smoking and taking drugs and eating too much or eating not at all or having pain in our bodies that puts us in room after room with doctor after doctor, acupuncturist and massage therapist and chiropractor, looking for an answer.

We avoid this by making our pain political and raging and lashing out at the news or the rumors of news or the latest flare in mass consciousness, yelling at the television or composing screes on social media and getting frustrated when the electric screens do not seem to hear us.

We avoid this by saying we are fine.

We avoid this, sometimes, by dying.

All these options are inevitable, really, and understandable when we truly take into consideration how much great pain we are in.

But there is something else. Prince called it "the afterlife." Some people count on that. But I am talking about a different kind of afterlife, a life after trauma. Here on earth. It is possible. I have lived it.

For moments.

This is the thing about time that I have learned as a survivor of trauma, and maybe it holds true for everyone really: There is no forever.

There is no then, or when.

There is only now.

And it is fleeting.

A butterfly, yellow and black, flitting under the oak tree in the west.

A hummingbird, hovering above the Rose of Sharon, red throat gleaming in the morning sun, using that throat to chirp a joyful greeting. And then leaving.
A bumblebee, bouncing on the fragile tomato blossom before taking her tiny feet into the flower and doing what she needs to do, not just for herself, but so we can, all of us here on earth, eat.

These moments of beauty, these glimpses of now, are all we have.

It does not seem like much.

But life is not about numbers and there is no way to do the calculation of the soul.

This is the work of literature.

Literature teaches us how to pay attention, and through stories and poems, we learn how to add the important things up in the end, and we realize just how much how much love and friendship and laughter and tenderness and beauty that there really is remaining in this life and in this world waiting for us to mend.

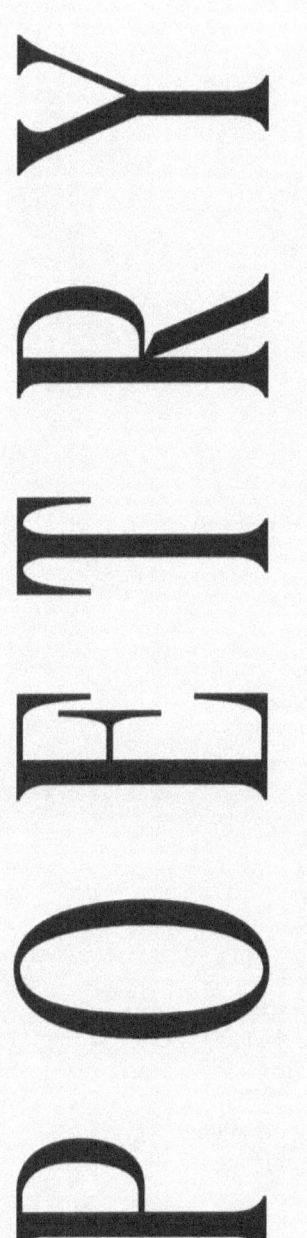

POETRY

ORIGINAL SIN

IF YOU KNOW, YOU KNOW

Annmarie Lockhart is the founding editor of two evolving poetry endeavors: vox poetica, an online poetry salon, and Unbound Content, an independent poetry press. A New Jersey native, she lives and writes two miles east of the hospital where she was born. You can read her words in fine journals online and in print.

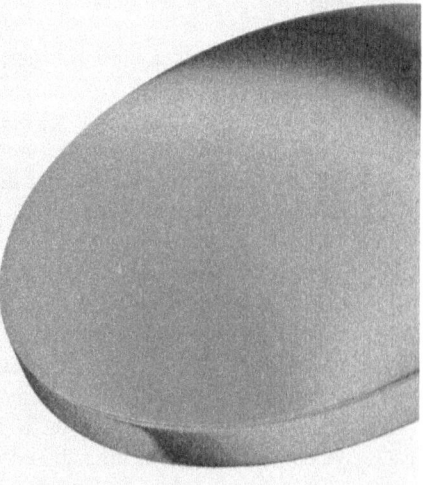

**ANNMARIE
LOCKHART**

Original Sin

The church got it wrong.
It wasn't Original Sin.
It was Original Hurt
that was the problem.

I think it was the forbidding
of the fruit that started it all.
What kind of god bans books anyway?
For God so loved the world
that he gave his only Son …
we all know what happened next.

Consider the hallmark traits of our species:
Cruelty, depravity, vindictiveness, avarice,
sanctimony, duplicity, and intolerance.
And let's review our legacy:

slavery, rape, arson, theft, murder,
displacement, forced migration, imposed
starvation, hoarding, redlining, blackballing,
cluster bombing, strip mining, name calling,
poaching, self-medication, mockery,
deception, denigration, betrayal

Don't think about it for long though.
Turn the channel. Keep scrolling.
The airwaves are humming 24/7
with Monday Night Football, reality TV,
true crime documentaries, TikTok dances,
how-to videos, and all the ads for all the things
we consume and consume and consume

just to keep us safe from confronting the trauma
we inherited and inflict while the world burns.

If You Know, You Know

The man who never eats leftovers
because he'd eaten too many raw potatoes
dug with his hands from fields that weren't his
when the Nazis invaded his country when he was a boy

The woman who forgets to feed her infant
and starves herself because she lost her mother
before she'd learned anything about feeding, nurture,
the way sustenance becomes survival and inheritance

The man who paints the complicity
of the church in the famine and searches for blood
on the internet, trying to find those who gave him away
to the nuns, so he can finish his own self-portrait

The man who never gets angry
because getting angry was dangerous where he grew up
in the shadow of the refinery, next to the cemetery that
flooded
and carried away the empty graves of his lynched neighbors

The girl who doesn't cry
since the day the guns came to school and rained
bullets down on a class of first-graders, their ABCs washed
away in blood on the pages of their marble composition books

The boy who will not go to school
in any of the towns his mom has moved him to, seeking refuge
from the bombs and the memory of his father, who joined the
army
at the start of the invasion and hasn't been heard from since

The baby who will never grow
up, her life stolen before she was born, her starving mother

reduced to scrounging for anything halfway edible she can find under
the ruins of their village, her heart heavier than her lifeless pregnant belly

No two traumas are exactly alike, but the body remembers, the heart perseveres, and the soul recognizes. If you know, you know.
The only question is, what do you do about it?

###

Annmarie Lockhart is the founding editor of two evolving poetry endeavors: vox poetica, an online poetry salon, and Unbound Content, an independent poetry press. A New Jersey native, she lives and writes 2 miles east of the hospital where she was born. You can read her words in fine journals online and in print.

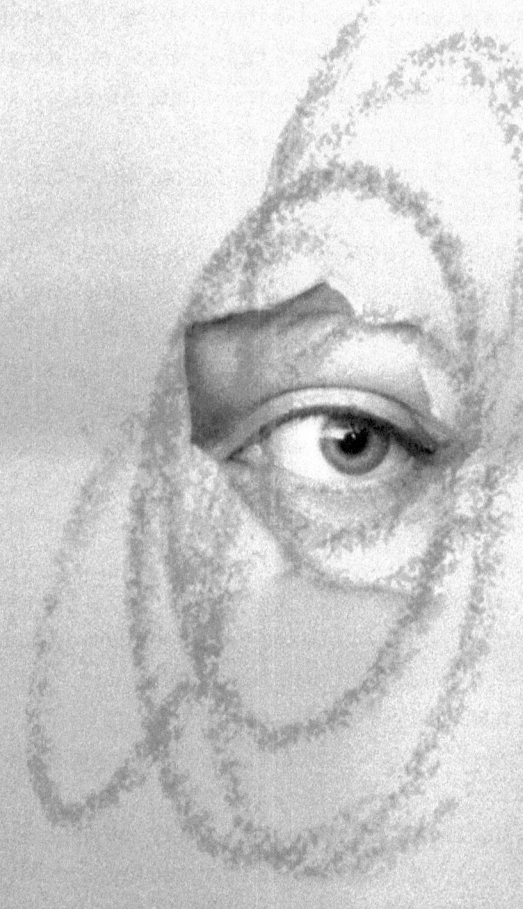

Manny Torres, originally from Brooklyn, NY, now resides in Atlanta, GA, where he works as a photographer, painter, and writer. Alongside "Dead Dogs," he's contributed to My Darling Atlanta, directed documentaries and music videos, and curated art exhibitions. His diverse career includes music programming, graphic design, insurance sales, and band management. Currently, he's editing crime novels and a supernatural western series. His debut novel, "Dead Dogs," is part of the Dog Trilogy, released between 2022 and 2023.

MANNY TORRES   THE HOTSHOT KID

Christmas in Philadelphia. Their first year here since getting married. Neither had lived in a big city since moving out of Florida. He'd had all intentions of getting that job drawing comic strips, but they'd landed here after the gold rush. After newspapers had slimmed down and everyone started reading their news online. At least that was the story he'd convinced himself of.

Paperwork snafu caused his methadone script to cut off, so it was back to the stoops, making friends with poison people. His wife's dowry—or whatever that was that her family had given them to purchase a house—went dripping down the vein drain. There were holes in his arms and in between his toes where all the spare change went.

"My people," Manx said. His arm around some old hopped-up lady. Not the usual bag lady who pushed her empty baby stroller up and down the block, but she looked like her. "Y'all my people."

"Y'all?" There was a huddle of them on the top step. Somebody was cooking and they stood arm-to-arm in a circle. They passed a fuming glass dick around, taking hits until it was drained.

"You ain't from around here, boy," some new guy said.

"What'a ya talking about?" Manx laughed. He had a small, goofy mouth, teeth all clustered together. His hair was long now, falling over his face. "I came here to run Philly."

The four or five of them laughed and called him names. He looked them up and down, seeing who was going to fix him. Hung out there an hour until it was his turn at the needle, and then wandered off into the night. Whatever that shit was hit like a brick, and that brick stayed lodged in his brain.

Snow fell, and the city would be smothered for a week. He vanished into the flurries. One of the stoop junkies looked up to see him disappear into the white wall of snow and hear his laughter.

"Hey, Frankie," Manx said. He ran into Frankie, AKA Stank Frank, AKA Dank Frank, at the corner bodega. "Hey, Frankie, lend me $200." Manx was lanky like a marionette, but Frankie was taller, always dressed like he was going ice-fishing in his earflap hat and scarf. Beady eyes, bulbous nose. Crustache. Suspicious of everyone and everything. Manx hooked onto his shoulder as he browsed the house cleaner aisle. Manx wore jeans, no socks, dirty feet in his old Converse. Slim leather jacket with sleeves too short, probably his wife's.

"The fuck I look like?" Frankie said.

"Hey, Manx," Rivera Jr. said from behind the counter. You could barely see his face, covered with lotto tickets. "Your wife was looking for you."

"What do you want $200 for?" Frankie asked.

"Come on, man," Manx said. "You know I'm good for it."

"You said you got off it."

"I did, I did. I just wanna tweak one last time, man. Come, on. One. Last. Time."

"You had a shot tonight, man. I can smell it on you."

"Come on, man. I'm good for it."

"No, you're not." Frankie grabbed some things and put them on the counter and paid for them. He nodded at Rivera Jr. and walked out into the snow.

Manx followed him.

Frankie looked at him over his shoulder. "Come on, get the fuck off."

They turned a corner and saw Losack walking across the street toward them.

"Losack!" Manx yelled.

Losack was a scrawny kid—28-year-old kid—with baggy jeans and tattered hoodie. Breath gracefully billowing above him. The sides of his bald head scarred up. Scraggly prison tats and a safety pin through his nose. Wearing his mother's parka and a Santa Claus hat.

"Whatchoo carrying, man?" Manx asked.

"Fuck off, man." Losack just wanted to get past them.

"You believe this fuck?" Frankie said. "He wants a hit after taking a hot shot. Unbelievable."

Losack stopped dead in the snow. "Oh, you holding?"

"I'm the only one holding on the block, asshole. Fuck you think?" Frankie was from Trenton, and you can relocate to Philly, but Trenton stays forever.

"Listen." Manx got excited.

"*Sshh*," Frankie said. "You'll wake up the block. Fuck's wrong with you? You're so goddamn loud when you get excited. You're worse than my kid this morning opening his fucking presents."

"You got a kid, Frankie?" Losack said.

They hovered around each other like hobos around a burning oil drum. "This guy," Manx said. "This guy, he's an *exemplary* family man."

Frankie didn't know whether he was joking or not.

"He takes care of his," Manx said. "Say, Losack, you wanna hit and go to Pamoa tomorrow?"

Losack leaned his head and looked at him with one eye. The white cotton ball of his hat dangled. "Why tomorrow?"

"It's closed today, man."

"What time?"

"I'm up early."

"It's 'cause you never sleep," Frankie told him. He was looking over his shoulder, their shoulders. Up the block, down the block. Couldn't see shit up the street on account of the snow.

"I sleep, man." Manx giggled.

"Ain't you married?" asked Frankie.

"Who, me?" Losack asked.

"Nah, this zombie next to you."

"Oh ho, yea," Manx said. His grin made him look cartoonish, like one of his drawings. He was a comics guy, but everybody knew him as Bodega Boy. "I got my little wife waiting for me back at the crib."

"Why you not there with her, instead of out here?" Frankie asked.

"I told her, I had to go out and find her something to unwrap. See, we have an *understanding*."

"Yeah, understanding."

"So, you gonna front me?"

Frankie immediately crossed the street, heading west. "Get the fuck outta here."

"So, we can't hit?" Losack said to Manx.

"Whatchoo got?"

"I don't know, man."

"Whatchoo mean, 'you don't know'? You carrying?"

"Yeah, but I ain't sharing."

"Aw, come on, man. Why you gotta be like that? It don't take but a grain. We can hit now, and then I'll get you tomorrow."

"I ain't running a charity, for you or for nobody. We can try to find something tomorrow. Let's save it for tomorrow, for the museum. You still drawing?"

"It's my life, man."

"*Weekly Gazette* get back to you?"

"Yeah, man," Manx said. "Real bummer, man. They said they found somebody else. Fuck those guys."

"That shit sucks, man. Didn't you and your lady move here from Florida for that?"

"Yeah, man. We did. We did. She's still painting and sewing. Make ends meet, you know."

"So, you working?"

"Not right now," Manx said. "I'm holding out for a management position."

Losack laughed. "Man, you can't manage nobody."

"Fuck you, man. So, we getting high?"

"Which one is it, man? Getting high or going to the museum?"

"You're the one holding, man."

"Tell you what, I can bring some Pinx. We can snort some."

"The fuck is Pinx?"

"Glitter? Pixie dust? Basically, I take my little sister's Adderall and crush it. Don't even have to step on it. Up your nose and it's pure clarity."

"Bet," Manx said. He twisted his hands and tittered. "Sounds good. Let me come witchoo, man."

"Bitch, I'm out getting some milk for my kid. And you high as fuck."

"Hahaha. Right, right. Okay, listen, come get me. Tomorrow. Throw rocks at my window if I don't answer. No, wait. Come down to Mayfair. I know some people. That's where I'll be."

"Don't you have a phone I can text?"

"Nah, man. I sold it. You know how it be. It's Christmas."

Next day, by the impetus of need and chemical dependence, Manx was back on the street with Losack by his side. Didn't know how he got there or where he was exactly. Sometimes he'd wake up on a stoop and wasn't sure what city he was in. *Jersey City? Staten Island?*

It was the morning after Christmas or the morning after that. Maybe. Wreaths, and lights still hanging. Discarded Christmas trees lined the curbs, which was always a way of saying, *good riddance,* especially with them still being decorated.

Christmas was over because the city was moving once again. The museum was open. Not that their plans fell into place, because he spent the morning fixing in a bodega bathroom. When he snuck out the back, Losack ran into him in the street. Manx reminded him about the Pinx. He waited while Losack went up to his mother's apartment, snuck into his sister's room, and took her meds.

They chased a bus and hopped on it. The city glittered like a block of ice. They both glittered. Everything was bright. Everything was cotton candy and special. Their chatter was constant, blending and bleeding to the point where they started and finished each other's sentences. Inside the Philadelphia Museum of Art was a large, mirrored piece that reflected their faces back at them a thousand-fold. And even their whispers came back to them, amplified from the concaved sculpture. They fumbled, tumbled, and laughed their way through the museum—until security discovered they hadn't paid admission and threw them out in the snow. They hung out under the statue of Rocky Balboa, but really on another plane of reality.

On their way back, they stole a bottle of cough syrup from a pharmacy that they passed back and forth until it was empty. They picked up a fully decorated Christmas tree left on the sidewalk. Limp and sad, but they ran with it, leaving a trail of tinsel and glass balls. They turned the corner on Ruffner St., near the Salvation Army and came upon three black men they referred to as the Three Wise Men: Crooked, Ish, and Glass. In their low-hanging pants, hoodies and parkas, leaning against a red brick wall, smoking.

"That Baltimore shit get you somersaulting," Ish was saying. "Like, you be trippin', but you falling, and falling, and falling backwards. Like that nitrous shit mixed with meth. Shit don't play."

"You don't know shit 'less you been had that," Crooked said. "Ask any nigga 'round here. Florida niggas, Atlanta niggas, Memphis niggas ain't got shit on this."

"What's happening?" Manx presented himself all fist pumps and gladhands.

They looked him up and down like the crazy white boy he was.

"Fuck you want, cracker?" Ish said.

"It's all good, son," Manx said. Laughing loudly and unruly, bumping up against them.

Losack looked worried. He was glazed, a ring of orange cough syrup circling his pale, cracked lips.

"No, it's not all good." Glass stood cloaked under his oversized team hoodie. There were burned bullet holes ringed with dried blood around his heart. "Don't be stepping up 'less you got paper, my man. This ain't EBT central."

Manx laughed again. "You wanna buy a Christmas tree? Still got the décor on it."

"Man, fuck outta here with that." Ish grabbed the tree from them and threw it across the street.

"That's a perfectly good tree!" Manx said.

"We Muslim, mufucka," Glass said. "We don't celebrate Christmas."

Losack looked at his sneakers and cleared his throat. He grabbed at Manx. "Let's go, man," he said.

"Nah, man, it's cool," Manx said. "These are my boys. *Ma niggas.*"

"Fuck you say, son?" Crooked yanked Manx by his collar.

Manx talked through the side of his mouth. "Nah, man, you know…you my boys."

"You lookin' for gravy?"

"Yeah, man. I'm down."

"Not if you broke," Glass said.

"But you know I'm good for it."

"No, you not," Ish said. "I know every mufucka you burned, *hoe.* Surprise you still walking 'round here with good legs. We know about your snatch-and-run shit. That shit don't play here."

Crooked shoved Manx into the street.

Ish came up and kicked Losack's ass and watched them run away.

They were three blocks down Ruffner when Losack stopped. "Hol' up," he said.

"S'matter, fuel running out? We can get more zizrup from the bodega on Reno."

"Let me catch my breath, dude. Shit. The fuck you runnin' on? Them dudes ain't playin'. You know anywhere else we can hit? You fuck with birria?"

"Ain't never had it," Manx said. "You got a man?"

"Maybe. For that shit, we gotta go to Jersey, though."

Manx looked anxious. Thumbnails bitten to the quick. Hands shaking.

"Hello?" Losack said. "Anybody in there?"

"Fuck, I think I see my wife."

They kept south and ran five more blocks before stopping. Stomping and slipping over slush.

"Is that Ernest?" Out of breath, Losack bent over and grabbed his knees.

"Where?"

"On the skateboard."

"Oh shit, there he go." Manx ran across the street, barely missing the cab that screeched and honked.

The Pakistani driver cursed at him.

"Sorry, brother," Manx said. "Yo! Ernest! C'mere. Let me shout at you, bro."

Ernest was a bear of a man. Mixed heritage. Maybe Honduran and black. Thick braids knotted close to his scalp. He wore a camo jacket and ripped jeans. And what looked like size-16 Vans.

Manx laughed. "Fuck you doing with that thing in the snow?"

Ern shot a cold stare over his shoulder. Losack was coming up behind Manx, but it was too late as Ern swung his skateboard around, smashing it into Manx's face.

"Whoa, man, whoa!" Losack's sneakers skidded to a stop. He spun around and ran off.

Ern bent down and lifted Manx by his collar.

Manx's eyes were uneven, staring in different directions.

Ern punched the center of his face. Again, and again. He stopped and dragged him through snow, dropping him against a building wall. *"You stupid, motherfucking piece of worthless dog shit! You motherfucking lousy junkie. Fuck right off. Go back to your mama down in Florida, you shit-ass piece of cocksucking shit!"* Ern beat him with every insult. He shook Manx and kicked him, then punched him again.

Manx could usually take a beating, but he wasn't getting up this time.

Ern walked off, holding his skateboard. "Merry Christmas, you dumb mufucka! You and your faggot-ass friend. That's a reminder, I ain't no charity. I don't give my shit for free, and your broke ass owes me."

Manx later woke up across the street, lying on ice, face purple and swollen, missing teeth. Dizzy as hell. Shaking. Snow was falling. He stood but slid on hardened snow and fell on his back. Hit his head hard. Snow covered him.

At the bodega, the young bride stepped in and asked around.

"Have you seen Manx?"

The counter guy shook his head. The guy watering the flowers at the bodega up the street told her no as well.

"You sure?" the young bride asked.

The man shrugged and pointed inside the store.

She went in, past the produce, past the soda display, and the Iberia products. Past the boxes of toilet paper and into the dingy bathroom in the corner. She opened the door, where she'd found Manx before, tied off, eyes rolled into the back of his head, drooling all over himself.

But he wasn't there.

She felt his presence like the dust of a ghost.

Tearfully, she fled, up three more blocks.

The girl at Arby's said no. The pizza place was closing but she went in looking for him. No one had seen him today. She checked the bathroom at the next place. And the next one. They watched her come in and all shook their heads when she asked.

She left without wishing anyone a Merry Christmas.

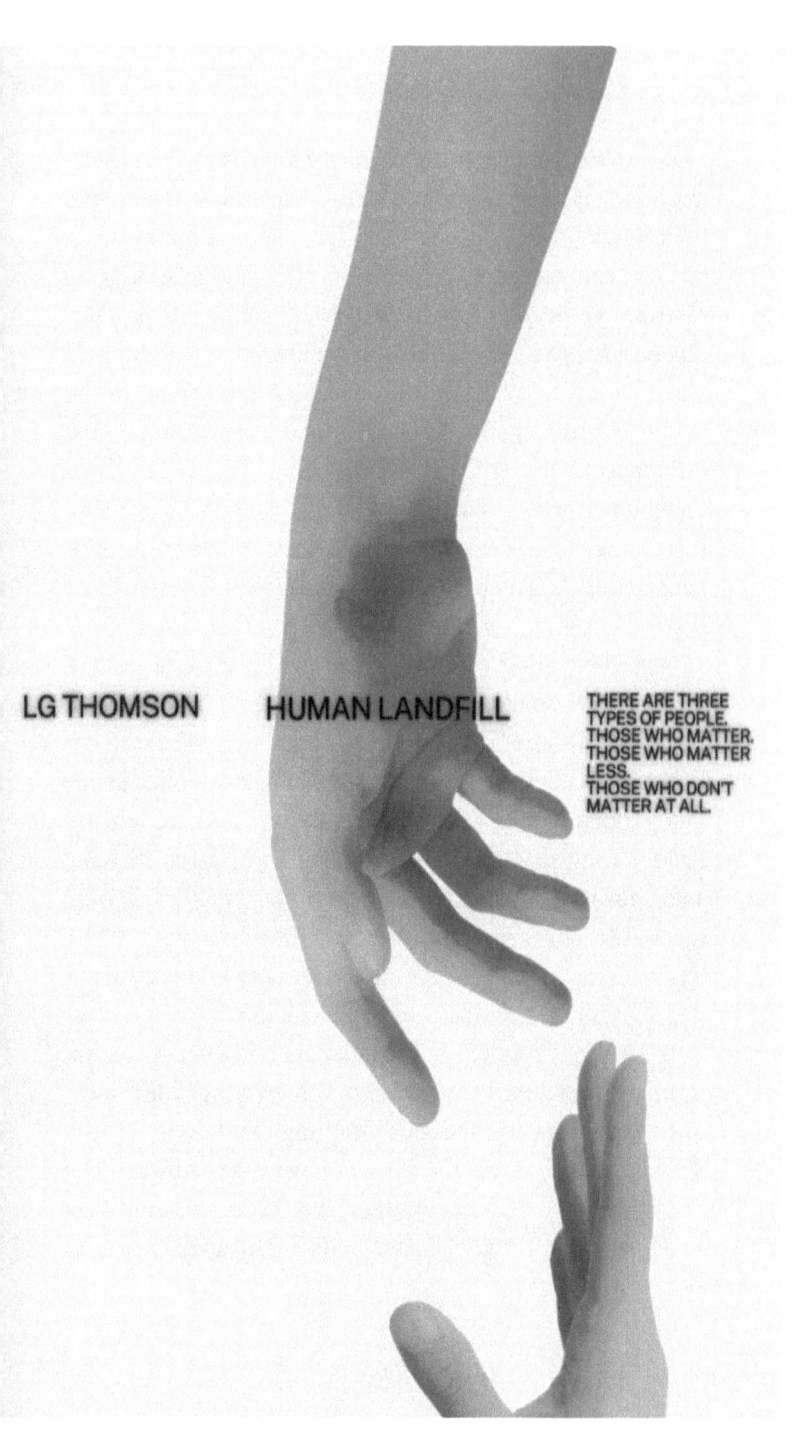

LG THOMSON

HUMAN LANDFILL

THERE ARE THREE
TYPES OF PEOPLE.
THOSE WHO MATTER.
THOSE WHO MATTER
LESS.
THOSE WHO DON'T
MATTER AT ALL.

Do you ever wonder what happens to the human detritus they clear from the streets? You know, the people the establishment sweeps away like maggot husks when the cleansing season is upon us. The authorities gotta sanitise, gotta keep the cities clean, shoot street dogs, poison feral cats and sewer rats, bulldoze the human trash clean out of the way. Gotta keep everything clean for the people who matter. The influencers behind the influencers, the chosen ones living in a world of understated plush and gloss. Don't want to be burning their retinas, churning their guts, scouring their consciences—if you can find them—with the stench of poor.

They don't want to see the men with matted beards who sleep under dripping bridges on beds of flattened cardboard. They want to be spared the pathos of hollow-cheeked women gesturing hand-to-mouth outside fancy delis while fine hams and rich cheeses cluster inside. They don't want to know that, if you wear the same socks for long enough, your skin will fester and scab over the cuffs, absorbing the rotting fibres into your filthy body. They don't want to see, hear, know about deprivation, destitution, dearth or drought.

What about you, who matters less than some, but more than others? C'mon, did you ever wonder, even once, what happened to those starving children in Africa? The ones you saw on TV when you were growing up. The ones your parents berated you about when you didn't eat your retarded dinner. Those kids with sharp ribs and distended bellies and flies crawling over their eyes as if they were dead and decaying already. Did you think they disappeared when you flicked the channel? Did you? Did you ever wonder if they made it?

I'll let you into a secret: They made it. Some of them. They made it here, scooped up and mushed in with all the rest of the human waste. Those starving kids from Africa are here, along with their feckless parents who didn't have the sense to be born somewhere better. Someplace with no artillery, no famine, no plague of locusts stripping everything to dust. Someplace that wasn't an earthquake zone, war zone, malaria zone, death zone.

The migrants are here too. Those small boat people with their big ideas and fancy notions about getting a job and a home to dwell in, food to eat and coin enough to send back home. Asylum seekers, economic seekers, greedy, cheeky seekers coming over here taking our jobs, looking for an easy ride on Benefits Street, sucking up our resources, eating our food, seducing our women.

In they flood, oozing into the gaps between our home-grown wastrels. Kids in care, chucked out the heartbeat they turn eighteen, let them take care of themselves. Kids fiddled by uncles, beat up by fathers, despised by mothers, pimped out by boyfriends. Used up, junked up, screwed up, bruised knees, dried jizz flaking on chin. Sharing the PTSD-loaded streets with ex-soldiers, screwed in the head, screwed by the regime they swore allegiance to, kids and warriors alike fucked by the system. Come cleansing season, they're swept out of sight, out of mind. Never knowingly remembered. Beat up, knocked down, spat upon, pissed on, scorned on and then forgotten because they don't matter.

All the forgotten are here.

All the victims are here.

HERE is a warehouse deep and wide as the Mariana Trench, situated beyond the back of out of sight, out of mind. Here is where *they* store chemical waste. Here is where *they* store us. Human landfill.

The famine-struck starving, the non-contributors, non-influential, economically unviable. The poor, sick, diseased, disabled, mentally unstable, emotionally deprived, born in the wrong place, wrong time to the wrong people, wrong coloured skin, wrong religion, didn't work hard enough, didn't try hard enough, underclass scum, othered, despised, dregs of the world. Useless eaters, all.

They ship us here and tell us we don't know how lucky we are.

That we should be grateful for the fetid air we breathe while they preach and preen from their ivory towers and gated communities.

The warehouse is immense, but we are many and, despite the vastness of the space, we are piled high like coal in a steamboat engine room, everyone rubbing up cheek to jowl, arse to elbow, choking on each other's fumes. There's no zoning, no classification, all is chaos. An eight-year-old girl with burn scars on her face—

refugee from a home turned rubble by a missile attack, lost her entire family in one blast—is squeezed between a man with a dog on a string and a woman with dead eyes.

The man with a dog on a string looks thirty years older than he ought, his soul broken by a priest with a taste for boys younger than ten. The dog is bone-skinny with gentle eyes. The woman on the other side of the girl creates a sick symmetry, being both as broken as the man and thin as the dog.

The trio are as typical and atypical an illustration of everyone crammed in here. Life's losers all and only ourselves to blame. We could have worked harder, tried better, aimed for mattering less instead of not at all, but none of us spun the wheel of fortune with the right kind of vigour.

Here's a fact: Funny thing about coal piled high, it starts to generate its own heat, its own beat. Maybe you can feel it already, a spark in the air, the temperature rising.

Here's another fact: There are more of us than there are of you.

Feeling that spark yet? Are you thinking about the moment that's coming? The moment when we ignite, when our multitude explodes into your world, a mega Vesuvius of discarded souls turning your skies dark, tearing up your plush, griming your gloss?

We are legion. United, the mass of us is more than enough to break down your gates, topple your towers.

These lowly worms are turning. The weak, the meek, we matter.

We're going to eat the rich.

Inherit the earth.

Share the wealth.

Can you feel the spark?

Poetry

To the Unnamed
Syrian Woman in the
Newspaper

David Hay

(2024)

A woman attempts to outrun the
colourless noise of violation, that
breaks landscape, tissue, bone. She is
wordless.
The syllables of blood melt into the air;
children's screams become as regular as
birdsong in the morning – maggots eat the
lines of breath and love is limited to a clichéd
line, and a retail assistant's exhausted sigh.

She flees in an unthinking fear, leaving her baby, by the
stump of a lemon tree, as a rhapsody of burning cinders
fall. Then the silence of endings of beginnings cups the
hollow cries of violence, melting dawn through her
impassive eyes. She screams and each person near is
ensnared by her despair that knows no border. Another
shot is fired, it releases heaven into her vacant eyes. The
covenant of grief is broken and all run, apart from the
unnamed woman who is denied history.

She stands as still as the horizon.

Poetry

Shiksha Dheda

The big, brilliant Woolf

I am all of you
1947 (India-Pakistan partition)

1875 (Indian indentured labourers
brought to South Africa)

The big, brilliant Woolf

- *After 'A room of one's own' by Virginia Woolf*

Don't call her *Mary Beton, Mary Seton, Mary Carmichael or
any other name,*
call her Virginia!

Call her Virginia and howl her name like a wolf
does to the
rare blue moon,

to the pack that tells it,
it belongs.

For a woman must have money and a room of her own.
Not just to write, not just to think,

but to feel, to express her ideas
- to love.

This is *the essential oil of the truth,*
that one should write what one wishes to write,
how one wishes to write it. Not for the fame,
nor for money,

but for the sake of writing
for *thinking of things
in themselves.*

Women, half of society,
have somehow,
been pushed to the fringes of society.

Undermined, suppressed,
voices taken away
- talent accredited to Anon,

but there is
no gate, no lock, no bolt that you can set upon the
freedom of the mind.

And so, we continue.

We continue to write,
to read,
to feel,

to love
· to live,
within and around ourselves,
surrounding our minds and hearts

with the rhythm of other women's bosoms,
standing on their giant shoulders,

making paths through the fields
splattered with the seeds of their patience,
watered with the blood of their battles.

Because ultimately who will,
who can,

who knows
how to *measure the heat and violence of a poet's*
heart, when caught and tangled in a woman's body?

Cw: mental illness, insinuation of possible death/war/PTSD

Poem for all the South African Indian women; giants on
whose shoulders I stand today

I am all of you
1947 (India-Pakistan partition)

I am a country
ripped apart.
Decimated.
Slaughtered.

One country
-two pieces-
-each the consequence of the other-
a home on either side abandoned
-lost, forsaken, demolished.

I jump on the back of a train
riding to ruination;
riding away from devastation
-my stomach a moving cocooned caterpillar-
birthing throngs of butterflies.

White butterflies weighed down by red rain.

1875 (Indian indentured labourers brought to South Africa)

I am a sardine.
Packed in a whimsical boat
-waddling through mayhem.

A mango slice
-sweet, succulent-
ricocheting in salty waters.

(continued)

Made to leave
-forsake my country-
-abandon my continent.

Desolate.
Destitute.

Marching to my watery grave
- reflections-
the mirrored pain of my fellow prisoners.

Present day/past/future

I taste the sugar cane in your salty sea water
some days.
I feel the anxious stroking of the wind on your back
as I board your train.
I look at my hands.
Your scars.

I speak.
Your language grabs my voice-box

          -spindly fingers-

                  scratching away at the
                fungus of colonial language.

I am you.

I am me.

I am all of you at once.

I am none of you at all.

Embracing Elle

Paige Johnson

Paige Johnson is co-owner of Outcast Press and author of the illustrated poetry books Percocet Summer and Citrus Springs. Most recently, her short stories are in the following anthologies: Cowboy Jamboree's MOTEL (about a counterfeiting couple on the run, unable to rest easy in a FL tiny home community w/ scuzzy redneck owners), Urban Pigs Press' HUNGER (a bulimic cam girl wishes she wasn't so lonely this Valentine's Day), Craig Clevenger's Put Out The Lights & Cry · Diner Noir (a lesbian couple blackmails men over fake rapes for money to start anew), and Anxiety Press' Mirrors Reflecting Shadows (about bi Miami sugar babies selling coke at a porn convention).

Dad will never recognize me like this: kohl eyes, a short black bob, and seven years taller. Seven years *made* a woman, despite having just scraped the age of 17.

Across the hotel lobby, he melds into the horde of businessmen. Their only resemblance to each other is a penchant for black, but if it weren't for his staggering height, I'd lose him.

I say to the man on my arm, "I-I'll meet you in the room. Got to freshen up." I point to my eyelashes. "I feel one of my falsies starting to fall."

The ogre frowns. Doubt etches dirty creases in his forehead. He must know: *Why would I return now that my pimp's been paid?*

I keep my brows from furrowing, despite the mounting pressure of time. "You didn't spend all that money to sleep with a droopy-eyed amateur, now did you?" I clutch his bulging bicep with an ounce of hate. "Look, I'll give you a show if you give me time." Even a minute's absence can make the heart grow fonder. I should know.

Before the biker bum can reach a verdict, I kiss the graying fuzz of his cheek farewell. *Dizzy 'em up,* that's what the more grizzled girls always told me.

Dashing from his grip, I promise myself that'll be the last frog I ever kiss. That I'll get away and come back for the girls who can't.

I tread miles of rust-colored carpet without spotting Dad again. I thought I was only yards behind, but even door-to-door questioning won't do any good. I can't harass 24 floors before my pimp finds out. The breath catches in my chest until I feel I've swallowed a ball of steel wool. Didn't think this heart could harden anymore, that anxiety could bloom any more barbs.

Half my life is spent fulfilling fantasies, but I never imagined I'd happen to book the same hotel as Dad. As bizarre as the circumstance is, I assure myself I didn't mistake his identity because I glimpsed the star tattoo behind his ear. Plus, it's likely his band would do a show in Atlanta. The Tabernacle is only three blocks away.

I wipe the baby tears from my eyes and start to laugh when a false lash falls with them.

The crack of a door stunts my giggle. "About damn time," my frog croaks. "Thought you ran off on me."

Broken clocks are right twice a day. I race down the hall.

The beer-bellied perv starts a beat behind.

We zip through the halls like we have a flight to catch.

I nearly crash into the cleaning cart—but slip into a closing elevator before he turns the corner.

I descend at a nauseating pace.

Curses and bangs sound overhead.

I choke back barf as I spill into the lobby.

Though I don't see the ogre aboard any of the candy-shaped capsules The Hyatt calls elevators, my heart pounds in my ears like his boots on tile.

"Lana!"

I was on the lookout for the wrong beast.

I lock eyes with my pimp. His eyes are snake slits, his face ruddier than a vulture's gullet. His fists clench with warning that would give me pause if the promise of shelter didn't seem so attainable.

≋ ≋ ≋

I hyperventilate inside a dressing room. A Baker Street boutique, that's where I inflate a plastic bag with woe. Footsteps outside the door keep me hot. Any pair of them could belong to my pimp. The devil has a name and I learned it when I was only ten years old: Dante, and his inferno is ignited by a sickness and greed attached only to numbers. He's obsessed with double-digits but nothing over 18, so I suppose my exit won't be as premature as my entry into sex and its (worry)work.

I'll never forget his cold, chapped hands and not just because they've crept upon me every night since. His overgrown pinky nail good for cutting coke or piercing fresh flesh. The thumbnail blackened from a dispute with a debt collector of sorts. The remaining nails curled and formaldehyde-yellow from rolling cigarettes. I'll never forget how they were uglier in action than appearance. How they pried me from a bright home strewn with giggly musicians and Mama's bohemian trinkets. How those skeletal hands delivered me to men with as sickly intentions.

I vomit into my shopping bag. Sweat glosses my face.

I don't dry my tears this time. I must erase this face. It too closely resembles Dante's target, his vision of a jailbait baby, a used-up Kinderwhore. It strays too far from the missing posters my family mourned over.

How do I reclaim that look, one of a babyface blonde who still possesses a hymen and a home?

Gritting my teeth in the mirror, I scratch away this garish imposter. I toss hair extensions into my sick bag, peel off lashes and specks of smoky glitter, rip out and apart my colored contact lenses. Maybe Lana the Grunt liked the faux-mod look, but Elle the Girl prefers a natural look, some color in her life—starting from the inside out.

Hope, that's a good look on anybody.

Pulling twenties from my push-up, I thank my john for one thing: being stupid enough to pay upfront. Steadying my breath, I strip. I mush my clothes into the mess bag and tie a knot. It's Lana's body bag now. Time for Elle to reclaim her voice.

"Hey, can I ask a favor?" I say to the clerks scurrying outside the door. "Some things to try on, please."

I turn from the ticket counter of The Tabernacle as an old girl—not a new woman. I spray-dyed my hair back to butterscotch, exchanged my backless gown for a more becoming fit. No more black. That's for death-obsessed adults. I'm all pink, the color of Mama's perfume, childish adoration spelled out in candy hearts, a new spring rising.

I wear high-tops now, not high heels. An A-line dress, not a G-string. The only skin I reveal is above the sweetheart neckline—It's only fitting that my chest be as bare as it's felt since puberty.

Unrecognizable to my enemies but an anomaly to this crowd of metal-heads, I pray the din of distant sirens means Dante suspiciously paced by the police station too many times in search of his renegade slave.

Either way, I'll kiss freedom in a couple hours—assuming I don't lose my VIP pass to pasty pickpockets. A smile crinkles my cheeks. It's contagious, as though the salvation of everyone around me also relies on Dad. Their arms are inked with his words, his face graces their shirts. They hold signs emblazoned with his stage name.

As spotlights fall on the curtain, they chant it. Dresden is the name of their messiah, but to me he's just Dad. Though "just" is no descriptor for the man who taught me the ABCs of English, poetry, and guitar. The parent I had to watch from afar after being snatched by someone with no song—only teeth and cacophony—to their soul. The dad I only knew through music videos and interviews on a hotel TV once Dante fell asleep.

Piecing my dad together from others' perspectives and dusty childhood memories is a pastime too painful.

What does my savior look like in the flesh, from the front?

My face warms with anticipation.

He rises from the smoke, a statuesque silhouette. As the veils drop around his feet, the balconies roar. Guitars don't just strum, they scream. The lights are angled to cast him as a dark angel. He's all grit and glam with rays emanating from obsidian hair, highlighting his war paint and rockstar stance.

I lean into the bunching sway of bodies, the sloshing of beer, the smell of weed. With all the combat boot-stomping, you could mistake this for a military coup. As the chords progress, black-lipped kids sing out of key. Tattooed teenagers shout choruses they must have memorized in detention. Or perhaps they learned the words while they shivered and perspired in a rollaway cot, trying to wean off amphetamines. Synth patterns could numb the nip of wolves for me, some nights.

I remember a writer from *Rolling Stone* scoffing that my dad makes music for trench coat kids and disillusioned Rust Belt waitresses. I can't help but snicker, wondering which group would claim me. I can't help but appreciate the kinship my dad kindles within this gamut of outcasts.

Every time he scans his rippling crowd of disciples, I wonder if there's a tidal pull to his eyes. Over

the cheers, lasers, and chugging guitars, can he sense
there's a section of the pit that needs more attention?

If parental intuition is real, could he recognize the
bone structure he took part in sculpting, the DNA he and
Mama weaved during their Jamaican honeymoon? Would
matching emerald eyes draw him in, make him question?

≷ ≷ ≷

Even if I can't be sure that that downward glance
from centerstage was for me, I know the finale was. It's
not often Dresden ditches his electric guitar and growling
for a bit of country crooning.

"The sun set on Brooklyn Avenue,
And wind scatters the story.
Newspapers rustle,
The milk carton cries,
But still, no one knows why.

"A man from Virginia,
A van off to Madison?
Tell me, Elle,
Who made you run?

"Mama leaves a light on
In a bedroom full of forget-me-nots
The camera boys want your freedom
But they're rolling out of steam

Seems that every season
Another blonde bird flies upstream

"I take the subway, see the signs
Yours is the only emanating light
Tell me, Elle,
Where did you sleep last night?

"May the mileage of your shoes
And the stamina of your smile
Carry you back home
Heaven knows that living out of a suitcase
Is worse when you're alone

"Where you've been, what you've seen,
We'll wash the memories clean
Tell me, Elle,
What you don't tell anyone,
You can tell me.

"Rusting bike wheels and
Sighs blown on dandelion spiels
Tell me, Elle,
That counting days instead of sheep to dream
Means we'll wake to more than distant screams.
Maybe this life isn't as hopeless as it seems."

Backstage, I shiver like a honeysuckle in the rain.
Despite my hot pink sleeves and stockings, I've gone

snow-cold. I never knew "cold feet" was a literal phrase, but I drag my Converse through tossed solo cups to get to the back couch. I shimmy through the poolhall haze, narrowly avoiding band members hypnotized by groupies with confetti still clinging to their cleavage.

On a brown settee, Dad sits alone, jotting in a moleskin. Apparently, I'm not the only soul skittish of approach. Leather pants, his coat's silver fur spiking his shoulders—it all oozes imposing. When my shadow dusts his boots, he looks up.

My heart clogs my mouth like an apple plugs a swine. My tongue squirms, throat tender. A deluge of water replaces words. Blubbering like a starstruck superfan, I turn redder than the Stardust makeup he scrubbed off in the shower.

Thousands of days apart and this is the best I can muster.

What about all the dress rehearsals in my head? Talk of how I've shoplifted his and Mama's CDs as self-addressed birthday presents for years. How I saved their *SPIN* cover-shoot and folded it into my sock for safekeeping. How I regret interrupting their studio sessions as a kid to fuss about a toy.

How, how, how have we missed so much and just reunited? How long until I can see Mama, the house, the cats, and call it normal again?

"I love you" is all I can say and it's scarcely audible, lighter than Mama's folk music murmurings.

I win a small smile. It's but a tug on his lips. He stands, wraps me in a hug. It's lukewarm fanservice. His bare chest smells of aloe and his jacket of crisp cowhide. I survey the foot's difference between us. Up close, you can tell he dyes his hair, silver threads peek through. Without makeup, his forehead is as lined as a mountain ridge.

He has to hide the white streaks and worry wrinkles I gave him seven years ago to remain in the public eye.

I feel like I could die—*should've* died.

"You don't get it," I start, scavenging for words that don't seem too shocking to say outright. "Splotchy hair and a handmade dress, don't I remind you of Mama?"

He squints his confusion, steps sideways. "Sorry, kid. I meet a lot of fans. I met your mama too? The club-owner in Memphis? You Dee's daughter?"

"What? No, no, I—" I stop before my tone can rise. What do I expect? My voice isn't even the same octave. "I— Step over here." I lead him to the hall graffitied Dirty South-style with jazz and blues players.

When I look back at him, his descending gaze is familiar in all the wrong ways. For all the lead-ons I've been forced to say, how could I not see the innuendo? That I come across as a shy starfucker?

My shaking must look like a Tourette's symptom.

"Well, what're ya trying to show me, li'l chickadee? Gotta line a women who want a share, so whatta ya say ya speed things up?"

My lips seem magnetized shut. This is like all the dreams where I can only spit up sand. In real life, all I produce are tears. More when he grips my shoulder with enough drunken force to make it shake.

He steadies up against the wall too, shoves a little metal bean up his nose and sniffs. He wakens a fraction.

My cheeks burn like his nose must. Even the light seems so wrong here, lecherous, illicit as the red of his septum implies. "You knew me before *I* knew me," I try, eyes wide with emphasis.

He slouches again against the burnt orange blocks of the wall, crosses his arms. Jack Daniel's peeks from his jacket pocket. "I don't know if that's supposed to be some dramatic teenage or Biblical bullshit, but I—"

"I-I'm Elle." My cheeks must be as pink as my dress, my voice as small as the lace perforations.

The height of his brows mimic mine. "You're *who*?" They come down hard.

"Elle. It's me, Elle. Daddy, I know it's insane. I just turned 17 and it feels like—" I clasp his hand, begging the memories to transfer through warmth. My words become bullet-fast: "I saw you at the Hyatt. It's me, I swear. Before then, I hadn't seen you since I was getting ready for school. You were right. Right about that Italiano in the van. On my way to the bus, he said he was a roadie of yours and—"

"There're easier ways to get your tits signed, kid." He throws up his hand like a stop sign—and *I* feel like I might vomit, chunk up his cowboy boots. "Fuck off," he says, hoarse and hardly there. Shaking his drooping head, he walks towards the den. "You already had my attention, didn't have to go and ruin it with some sick prank!"

"What? What?!" My volume snags eyes from the next room. "Y-You sang, 'Elle, tell me what you don't tell anyone' and h-here I am." My eyes narrow, using all their puppy dog might to spool him back into place. I jog up and yank his arm. "Dad, I mean it."

"Miserable cunt, go sell your story to *Inside Edition*—"

"Elle. I'm really Elle. You should know. You named me." I fight his head-shakes with facts. "Yes. In Negril. I was planned. Mama wanted to conceive before she was 27. Something about bad luck with singers and that number. You joked I was your rasta baby. Even said so to my English tutor the day before you recorded in Jamacia. Miss Abbot in Greenwich, remember?"

His lips straighten from their grimace. "H-How do you know that?" Eyes hard as jade. "Listen, if ya don't back off, I'm gonna call—"

"Is Lars still your bodyguard—even though you think his wife wants you? Even though you said to Mama they both smell like stale potpourri? Is that proof enough that I'm who I say? Look." I scratch at my ears, unclasp the jewelry. Gold, little daisy earrings he bought me in the Philippines. I display them on my palm like they'll overshadow seven years' distance. "Ask anything you want. I'm your girl."

Words leave his mouth as air. His argument a ghost.

I impale his pause with all the evidence I can muster. "And I know Mama *hated* her fifth anniversary gift. It was a ring that never left its box, so there're no photographs. No interview mentions. It was a pewter snake with diamond eyes. She threatened to pawn it the Easter you toured through Europe with that girl group. Toxic Twins or Twisted Tiaras, something silly like that. Damn it, she was jealous."

His gaze shuffles between my face and the custom earrings. He's as white as he appears in-concert, swaying with…uncertainty? He'd call for help if he could.

My stomach scrunches. I was never religious, but pray, pray, *pray*.

There's a break in his veneer, I just have to jab the crowbar in.

I bite my lip before delivering another painful reminder. If only what sears wasn't so memorable. "It wasn't just tabloid gossip. She was as jealous as you'd get over her bassist. That wannabe-Bowie with the white eyeshadow. Admit it, you always suspected she had a fling with him. You wrote an unreleased song called 'Mood Operator' about how he'd always pit Mama against you. I found your notes for it while searching for homework."

He can scarcely stay upright, tongue clucking with all he can't articulate. "Elle?" is all he keeps asking, like he's talking to an apparition.

I know it's a lot to process. Especially after that bottle of booze he downed on stage and spit all over fans like me. I nod and nod like he's still ballading. On this rocky roll, I keep spitting out facts, proving *me, me, me*: "Y-You're afraid of dogs, even yippy ones because one bit you so bad in kindergarten, you had to have a leg grafted. Every Sunday, Mama and I'd pick flowers for our hair. We'd feed rabbits with the carrots we grew in the garden. Once, in second grade, I got sent home for bringing your scorpion pipe to show and tell. I thought it was a whistle."

Something breaks behind his eyes—our eyes—besides the reservoirs. He lunges forward, searches my face for credibility, grasping.

I laugh through a stream of tears. "The cheeks resemble Mama's, huh?" Our noses aquiline, brows thin, complexion ruddy under the eyes.

He pulls my lips back like inspecting a horse. Same side snaggletooth as before.

Final test. He crouches, touches my knee, wobbles. I step back and peel down the tall sock for him.

"I told you," I murmur, pointing out the tiny scar. "From smashing into Aunt Rita's coffee table. During a game of tag with Li'l Charlie. Listen, I'm no phony. Not a sham of a fan. *Listen*. Like I did to you."

"Elle," he cries, picking himself up, then me, from the floor.

This embrace obliterates the last, the dread of rejection and a life better lived in print. Squeezing seven years' space between us, we smile like sadists as the last of our makeup bleeds down our faces. We smile, grateful to have the next seven years to cut the stitches from the wound, the string from our masks.

"Elle, it's really you."

BRENDAN HENEGHAN

Ghosts of Sonara

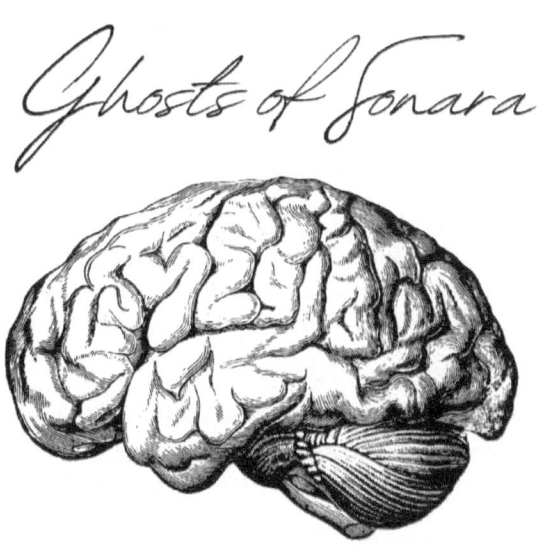

BRENDAN HENEGHAN

"What did I sign us up for?" Jonathan asked me as we barreled down the dark and dusty road.

"Beats the hell outta me," I replied.

"We could very well die out here."

"No kiddin', Johnny Boy, but it'd come from a snake bite. There's enough water in this backpack to last us a week. We both have enough food to last even longer. But no phone connection."

"Don't call me that ever again," he chuckled. "Just have to watch our steps. If we do fuck ourselves over, we can hike the ten miles back to the highway if we, God forbid, can't find the truck. We're stocked on provisions. Besides, Brendan. I'm from West Virginia. This ain't my first risky descent into the wild."

"Bro, don't even try to hit me with that Mothman bullshit."

"I saw it!"

"Yeah, and I had a run-in with Tainted Keitre in the swamp back in Louisiana. Bastard gave me a sip of whiskey out of a human skull."

"Enough banter, you Irish degenerate. We have a mission to accomplish. Make no mistake, this is unforgiving land."

"Don't have to tell me twice. JOHNNY BOY."

We had awoken in Phoenix at 3:30AM to prepare for the trek. It was 4:46 when we left the truck in an open space, near the foothills of the Sierra Estrella Mountains. Saguaro cacti stood against the rising sun, dark silhouettes like prophets reaching to Heaven. Ten miles of uninhabited desert barred us from the nearest paved roads. Ocotillos, elephant bushes, and chollas stoically rested at the foot of Hayes Peak. Other than my companion and me, no human beings could be found for an unknown number of miles. Ghostly silence across the sparsely inhabited Gila River Indian Reservation.

Although they lay in the Sonoran megacity's backyard, nobody in Phoenix talks about the Sierra Estrellas. There are no trails, markers, or signs. It's a barren badland ruled by Mother Nature and the Supernatural. People are known to go missing in those hills. This is the same lonely mountain range where UFOs were spotted during the Phoenix Lights in March of 1997. The last known location, before vanishing. Tales of Spanish gold and bloody conflict between warring local tribes illuminate the ominous vibrations unique to the mountains. Neither of us were aware of these stories at the time.

For over an hour and a half, we hiked up the ridge. Record time. Lightning across the mountain. Jonathan said I climbed with the agility of a wolf. To that, I released a savage howl, reminiscent of our pre-Roman Briton and Hibernian forebears. We both trace our lineage to the Lands of the Midnight Sun. But that desert was our adopted home, having left the east, where our families chose to settle generations ago.

Pink, orange, and purple clouds rolled in across the blue sky and the landscape looked like a classic western painting. The wicked wind howled an eerie song.

Mixed with our footsteps and singing birds, the land rang silent otherwise. We scaled large boulders, crossed dry riverbeds, and penetrated further into nothing. Until the noise stopped. No more birds. Wind gusts faded into the silent void.

"Do you hear that?" Jonathan asked me.

"No, but wait a minute," I replied.

We paused. My ears listened.

OOOOOAAAUUUUHHHH...

"Yo, what the FUCK is that?" I whispered.

"I don't know, man. I don't like this."

"Maybe it'll go away. We should be very glad I have this." I unsheathed the machete Max Woodruff gave me before leaving Covington in June. We came prepared. Jonathan is an experienced woodsman. I know a thing or two myself, but he's just different, to put it plainly.

The moan chilled my blood. He seemed concerned but unbothered. Neither of us could identify it. We doubted the possibility of a big cat. If it was, we wouldn't hear it. At least until it came within a few yards. Besides, a single human voice is capable of scaring panthers from far off, even causing them to abandon a meal. But what if the noise came from something else? Something neither man nor beast?

Fifteen minutes passed and no moans. We shrugged it off. We scaled a series of dark boulders across black crevices that no rational person would dare descend. This was the only viable path toward Hayes Peak. We hopped from boulder to boulder.

Jonathan took point, and he turned to me, pale as a ghost, eyes wide like he'd caught a glimpse of the fires of Hell. He had stopped in his tracks. "Brendan..." he whispered.

"Jonathan, what's behind that boulder?"

"Look... Very slowly and be very quiet..."

"Dude, tell me what the fuck is over that boulder."

"Something dangerous. But we should be safe from here."

"Okay..." I crept forward and peered over into the dim pit. About seven or eight feet below, a rattlesnake glared back at us, coiled and in a striking position. It fucking rattled. Until then, neither of us had ever stared directly into a rattlesnake's eyes. It was greenish brown, spotted, and must've been three to four feet long. There was more. The serpent rested atop the remains of what once was a coyote, now reduced to bones and dust. The skull was clearly canine.

We slowly backed off the boulder to search for an alternate route. I imagined the snake speaking. It said, "Human beings are the only creatures on earth who must leave home to seek home." This funneled me into a philosophical whirlwind over the human condition, and how we are domesticating ourselves to death. We have lost the savage, primal grit that once defined our species. This dry desert that commingled with life and death, the heathenism of merciless terrain, and ghosts of subjugated peoples and traditions, froze the blood in my veins. It was a place of perdition. Forgotten and surrendered to the animals and a harsh revenant. These wandering thoughts didn't last long.

Jonathan had an idea. A simple and juvenile one.

"I think that snake was a warning," I said.

"Same here," Jonathan concurred. "I'm getting some kind of 'do not enter' message from it. I'm not sure if I wanna keep going. Part of me wants to, though. We have to settle this. "

"I know we agreed on finding another route. But this is bad voodoo, like we're trying to cheat nature. I think you and I both know how that usually goes."

"Mhm. We'll have to keep this simple. This is Native land. We're on a reservation. As much as I'd like to do some rocking-throwing competition, you never touch anything out here unless you have to. Rock paper scissors. If you win, we head back to the truck. Best of three. No re-dos."

I won, choosing rock and paper.

Although neither of us verbalized it, relief encumbered our spirits. Something about those hills creeped us the fuck out. We both considered the snake a bad omen.

"Venture further and something bad will happen," is something else I imagined the snake saying.

The nearest hospital is two hours from the foothills, and we had a hefty hike down the ridge. The snake and carcass played with our heads. We had completely forgotten about the moans.

OOOOOAAAAUUUUHHHHH!!!! It returned, louder and nearer.

I heard it clearly this time. I tightened the red cloth I wore Apache-style around my head and firmly gripped the machete, still unsheathed and ready to pierce and hack bone and flesh. From a young age, my father taught me how to wield a blade—mostly buck knives, but I had a wooden sword that never left my side between ages seven and ten.

We spotted the truck about a mile away. In an orderly fashion, we embarked on our descent, over more boulders, crossing the bone-dry riverbed, and discussing what the hell made those noises. Jonathan remained steadfast, theorizing that a large cat was stalking us. I was skeptical. To tell the truth, I hoped it was a big cat, because the moans sounded unlike anything I'd ever heard.

The truck never seemed to get any closer as we cascaded down the foothills. The moans persisted and, by the time we were half a mile from the truck, they intensified.

"I have a bad feeling, Brendan. I have a really bad feeling."

"Explain."

"I think we're being watched. Followed. You feel that?"

"Not so much, but the noises make it pretty clear." This was a lie. "I've been suppressing it."

"We need to get back to the truck."

"Damn right, we do." Sweat covered my bare back. The idea of facing whatever the hell was following us so close to the truck whooped me into terror. My heart rate spiked. I swigged some water, and we pressed toward the vehicle.

Ten minutes later, the voices came.

"Okay, Brendan, are you hearing what I'm hearing?" Jonathan asked again, his face painted a ghostly white.

"No."

"I heard people talking."

"People?"

"Yes. Hello?"

Silence.

We're leaving!" Jonathan shouted.

"Dude, you cannot announce to the world that we're pissing our pants!" I scolded.

He shrugged.

My heart pulsated. A dreadful, deathly feeling swept over me. If Jonathan did in fact hear voices, and nobody responded to his calls, whatever was there was not friendly, but hostile. They did not want their position revealed. *This is the rez, this is the wilderness*, I thought. *We are not welcome here.*

"OOOOOAAAAAUUUUUHHHHH," the moan reverberated over us, but this time it was not beside us, behind the rocks and shrubs.

"Fuck, dude," Jonathan shakily muttered. "That came from the truck."

"Don't say that. Don't you fuckin' say that!"

"I'm not kidding, Brendan. All I have is a knife. Be ready to use that machete."

"Jesus, man! Knock that shit off, you're freakin' me out! I grew up around swamps and never been this fucked up… I'm ready for anything."

"I know," he said.

I was not interested in admitting he was right. I allowed fear to cloud any and all desire for truth. Anyone who understands human psychology in the slightest knows that too much fear shadows all truth and judgment. My heart was going to explode.

The noises drew closer and closer from behind the foliage and echoed through the mountains.

We had no choice but to press on. This went from a fun adventure to a potential fight for survival. Within minutes, we returned to the truck. Salvation! To our relief, it was solitary: no creatures, ghosts, extraterrestrials, or homicidal desert maniacs in sight.

Someone or *something* was stalking us. It wasn't until that night that I discovered an article from 1999 about three botanists who hiked up into the Sierra Estrellas. They heard the same noises. Online forums also discussed the desolate and possibly supernatural phenomenon. One thing remains certain: We followed our guts and made the right choice, abandoning our three-hour mission.

We peeled off down the dusty road and didn't look back.

His Last Monsoon

Amy Ward-Smith is an Australian writer from the coastal town of
Tweed Heads. She spent several years living and traveling in
Southeast Asia but three kids, two cats and ridiculously overpriced
rent means she doesn't get to travel as much as she'd like to these
days. Her short work has been published in various literary
magazines and anthologies. She's currently trying to piece back
together a novella ten years in the making, that she cut up with
scissors (literally, in the true sense of the word).

Amy Ward-Smith

12 July 2009.

We landed in the middle of a monsoon downpour. The plane shuddered as it descended into Wattay Airport. Outside, it was too grey to glimpse the city that would be my new home.

The tiny airport had no connecting bridges, so I emerged into the deluge via the uncovered stairs, holding tight to the rail. An umbrella in the monsoon season might have been a wise idea.

Inside, the airport was quiet. I handed over my passport and some US dollars to the friendly man at the Visa on Arrival office. A few minutes later, it was handed back, visa stuck inside, and I passed through, officially on Lao soil.

The organisation I would be working for had said they would send someone to meet me at the airport. I fished out the glasses I'd taken off in the rain, attempted to clean them with the bottom of my shirt, and scanned the arrivals area, spotting a man holding a sign with my name of it.

"Liv?" He smiled and lowered the sign as I approached.

I nodded.

"I'm Kham. Your new coworker."

"Nice to meet you."

"Come. I take you to where you stay."

I followed him out to the carpark. It had stopped raining, and the sun was threatening to appear from behind the clouds. Patches of blue broke out. The slight dampness on my skin from rain quickly turned to sweat.

We arrived at a Jeep that looked almost as old as Kham. I glanced at him as we pulled out of the parking lot. He appeared to be in his late-20s. His black hair was cut just above his ear, swept over to one side, apparently untouched by the rain. The sun emerged and he pulled out a pair of imitation Ray-Ban Aviators.

"Is this your car?" I asked as we drove through streets more populated with motorbikes than any other type of vehicle.

"No. It belong to our work. I just drive sometimes."

"Sorry you had to come all this way and get me. I thought they would just send a driver or something."

Kham laughed. "Not too far. Soon you will see. Vientiane's a small city. Nothing is very far."

"Are you from here?"

"Lao, yes. Vientiane, no. I come from the village, further north."

We pulled up at a guesthouse on a street so narrow, the Jeep took up almost the whole road. Kham insisted on helping with my backpack. "I pick you up tomorrow to go to the office," he said before leaving.

"It's not necessary."

"No worry. Just 'til you know where to find it."

Kham departed, and I went upstairs and washed off the mixture of rain and sweat on my skin.

13 July 2009.

Sunlight danced on the pavement, filtering through the mix of French colonial buildings, Lao-style houses, and construction sites as I sat outside the guesthouse on the street, drinking too-sweet coffee and watching motorbikes buzz past. Female passengers (wearing the intricately woven Lao skirts called *sinh*) sat with both legs hung to one side as they texted on their phone or talked to the driver. I wondered how they managed to balance like that.

Kham pulled up, not in the Jeep, but on a small motorbike. "You okay on motorbike?" He handed me the spare helmet.

I nodded, thankful that I'd decided to wear pants.

There's a strange, uncomfortable intimacy about being on a motorbike with someone you barely know. Trying to keep in flow with the driver, not to throw them off balance, but at the same time not wanting to lean too close to the body of a stranger. Especially when the stranger is an attractive one.

We pulled onto a road that appeared to be in the process of being paved. The office was in a colonial-style house with whitewashed walls that had seen better days.

Inside, I met the other six staff. Anna, my supervisor, briefed me in her office: "Don't talk about politics. Especially not in public places. Avoid telling people about your work. Tell me immediately if you feel you are being watched or followed, or if anything strange is going on." Anna paused, looking down at the pen she was spinning between her fingers. "This is not Australia, or even Bangkok. The government isn't our biggest fans but, for now, they tolerate us if we play by their rules and stay in line. But it's best to keep in mind that we're always walking on shaky ground."

As the day went on, it became clear that Kham wasn't just someone who drove foreigners around. He was the heart of the organisation.

09 August 2009.

I settled into the slow rhythms of life in Vientiane. Work was interesting but largely uneventful. The restrictions placed on NGOs meant a lot of effort to achieve small goals, and we were always watching our backs. Despite this, the Lao capital felt remarkably safe and calm. The threats were quiet, hidden, lurking just beneath the surface.

Though Kham had insisted he would only help me get to work for the first few days, I found him waiting at my door each morning. After the first two weeks, I started accepting his help without argument. On rainy mornings, we'd both don our ridiculous garbage-bag-like raincoats, arriving at work drenched just the same.

I was still nervous with every ride, cautious not to lean too close, fearing the surge of energy whenever I touched Kham's body. Getting involved with a coworker—my boss, really, although he never called himself that—was a bad idea itself. Getting involved with a Lao coworker was an even worse one. I'd read the warnings before I came about the laws against sexual relationships between Lao citizens and foreigners unless they're married. So, I tried not to slide too close—a difficult act on a small motorbike.

Sometimes, we went out after work to eat and drink together: Kham, Anna and the other staff. But one Sunday, I was alone. I wandered along the banks of the Mekong. The sun hung low over the river towards Thailand. A clear afternoon, but the dense, humid air held the constant threat of rain.

Heading home, I saw a familiar face pull up in front of me on a motorbike.

"Hey. Where you going?" Kham took off his sunglasses and smiled.

"Just going home. What about you?"

"Hop on. Let's go drink."

Kham drove down to the southern end of the road along the Mekong. He parked the bike, and we walked down to one of the simple bamboo shacks that lined the water. There were no other customers.

We sat cross-legged on the floor in front of a low table, and ordered Beer Lao, which, as usual, was served warm, accompanied by a bucket of ice. Kham dropped a couple of ice cubes into each glass. His elbow bumped my arm as he poured the beer.

A hoard of mosquitoes buzzed around us. In the distance, the sun melted into the river.

"You don't talk much," Kham said as he sipped his beer.

"Sometimes there's not much to say."

"Do you mind if I smoke?"

"No. Go ahead."

He lit up, taking care to blow the smoke away from my face. He made small talk, asking about my family, my life in Australia, the work I'd done in Thailand before coming here.

The inevitable downpour arrived, its noise driving us back towards silence.

The waitress bought more beer. The patterns woven into her *sinh* rippled like the river as she walked away. The rain enveloped us in a blanket of grey, separating us from the world. Droplets snuck through the thatched roof, dampening our skin and hair. Kham's hand crept towards mine, our fingers finding each other and intertwining. We stayed there until the rain stopped.

28 August 2009.

We went out for Anna's birthday dinner. I hadn't seen Kham much since that Sunday a few weeks prior. He'd been working on projects in various provinces. Anna said he was currently in Khammouane and was unlikely to make it back in time for the party.

We went to a nice Lao restaurant, close to the river just outside the city centre. Anna ordered a lot of dishes to share: whole fish deep-fried with garlic and chili, grilled beef with spicy tomato dipping sauce, fried frog legs, Luang Prabang sausage and of course *laab,* the spicy mince salad that was the national dish. The Beer Lao flowed as we tried to talk about anything other than work in the dimly lit restaurant.

We'd almost finished our dinner when a slim figure appeared at the end of the table.

"Kham, you made it." Anna jumped up and greeted him.

"Happy birthday, sister." Kham handed her a small gift and sat down at the empty chair at the end of the table.

The familiar tension came back. Though Kham was a few seats down from me, I became conscious of every movement, every word I spoke.

Dinner finished and we went out to the carpark. Kham lit up a cigarette and put his hand on Anna's shoulder. "More beer, birthday girl?"

Anna shook her head. "I've had enough."

Kham turned to me. "How you going home?"

"I'll just take a tuk-tuk."

"Come." He waved towards his bike. "I'll take you."

Kham had forgotten the spare helmet so insisted I wear his. We rode towards the city. The night was unusually cool, and I leaned into him to steal some of his warmth. We drove past dark houses in alleys with no streetlights, before turning onto the better-lit main road.

The beer had made me relaxed, distracted. I didn't look ahead. I watched the other motorbikes go by, the bright lights blurring in the night.

The bike slowed without warning. Kham's body stiffened. All his warmth drained away.

Up ahead, a policeman waved us towards the checkpoint on the side of the road.

We both got off the bike. The policeman spoke to Kham in Lao.

I tried to figure out what they were saying.

Kham handed over his license and registration papers.

They spoke some more.

I gleaned that the policeman, who appeared drunk, was asking for a bribe for the offense of not wearing a helmet. *Beer Lao money.*

Kham handed over 20,000 kip. Less than $2.50.

The policeman sent us on our way.

"Let's go get a drink," Kham said as we got back on the bike. His body still felt cold.

He pulled into a quiet bar playing Thai love songs.

We sat opposite each other. The small candle on the table flickered. Kham seemed distant.

"Are you okay?"

"I don't like checkpoints."

"But nothing happened?"

He looked away, into the darkness. His fingers picked the label on the beer bottle. Insects flitted around the light above, vying to get themselves electrocuted.

30 September 2009.

The weekly staff meeting. Anna ran through the usual business, asked, "Kham, you're going to Luang Prabang next week?"

Kham nodded. "I think I need some help on this one."

"Take whoever is needed."

Kham didn't look at me. "Liv never been to the field project before."

Anna nodded and ended the meeting. She asked Kham to stay. I heard her speak to him in Lao. My language skills still weren't good enough to understand what she said.

7 October 2009.

We'd driven up to Luang Prabang in the Jeep. Though the distance from Vientiane was only around 300 kilometers, the trip through the winding mountain roads took over 10 hours.

After finishing work at the field project, we were meant to return to the guesthouse in Luang Prabang, but

Kham wanted to show me his village, which was less than an hour drive.

"Won't your parents be surprised if you show up there with me?"

"No. My mum okay. She won't mind."

We drove through the mountains to an ordinary-looking Lao village. Kham stopped at a house in the centre and briefly went inside while I waited in the car.

When he returned, he looked disappointed. "My mum not there. But I got keys from my uncle."

Kham's house was on the outskirts of the village. A beautiful teak house overlooking the mountains. It wasn't large but it was more impressive than most of the homes we had passed by.

Though it was still afternoon, there was already a chill in the air. There was a large deck at the back with a wooden daybed. Kham dragged some folding triangle mattresses and blankets out for it.

This strange aloneness—this rare feeling of it just being us—made us shy. We sat against the cushions, together but apart. Not touching. Not speaking.

"Is it okay, me being here?" I asked after a while.

"What you mean?"

"I mean, will we get in trouble?"

"No. My uncle is Chief of the Village. We're safe. No one going to make trouble."

"Where are your parents?"

"My mum gone to the north. Visit her relatives." He paused. "My dad died. Five years ago. Pneumonia."

It struck me that I'd never dug this deep before. I'd never asked about his family. Everything between us was all silence and absence.

He turned to me. "Why did you leave Thailand? Why come here?"

"Bad relationship. It all became a mess. I needed a new start."

He laughed. "So, you came and found even bigger mess?"

We were lying down now. His face was close. I could see each one of his short, dark eyelashes and the shades of brown in his eyes.

"Aren't you scared?" I asked.

"Now?"

"No, I mean, because of your work?"

"Are you?"

"Yes, sometimes. But I have the Australian Embassy to help me. I don't think the government wants to get involved in a major diplomatic spat. But you only have your government."

Kham shifted closer to me. "All the time. Every day. I'm scared."

"Don't you ever think about going somewhere else? Leaving all this shit, all the fear behind."

"This shit is my shit. This my place. I'm meant to be here." He closed his eyes, and I breathed in his skin. His hair. Kham sat up. "Enough sad talk. You want to smoke?" He pulled out a small bag of weed he'd gotten from his cousin and rolled a joint.

We passed the joint back and forward. The mountains faded away and it was just us, legs tangled together, happy, lingering between dream and sleep.

Somewhere, in the distance, a gecko called out for its mate.

30 October 2009

Most nights back in the capital, Kham came to my room. Unmarried Lao citizens were not allowed in a foreigner's room, but the receptionist knew us well enough to turn a blind eye. Things were different, though. The intimacy that had grown between us in his village was drowned by the fear, the silent oppression that lingered beneath the city. He touched me softly, hesitantly, as though he may disappear at any moment. His body grew stiff, and he made love with increasing urgency, without pausing, lest the invisible demons that haunted him might catch up.

In the mornings, he returned to the person I knew: tender, smiling, light-hearted. Relieved to find the new day. At work, he remained passionate and seemingly fearless. Sometimes, when he left the city on a project, I wandered the quiet, muggy streets alone, my body aching, searching, longing for the mountains, for that small space we'd carved out, no matter how briefly, that space in which we could be ourselves. For the mist of his breath in the early morning air.

I recalled the sight of him bathing, tossing the cold bucket of water over his head, a shiver running down his spine. His hair, lengthened by the water, hanging almost to his shoulders. Drops of water clung to his light brown skin, his slim muscles glistening. Light filtered through the vent on the wall, striping his body like a solitary tiger.

I leant against the bathroom door, still wrapped in a blanket.

He turned to me. "Come on."

I shook my head. "It's too cold."

"Cold water good for you." He took my hand. The blanket dropped to the floor.

Goosebumps rose on my skin before the shock of the cold water even hit me. For a moment, I felt numb, but he pulled me towards him and I shivered into his smooth chest, smelling the soap on his skin. Outside, the unfamiliar sound of birds—conspicuously absent from the city—greeted the morning light.

05 November 2009.

We were meant to go out for drinks with the rest of the staff, but we got lost in some back lanes along the way. Though the city was small, we'd never ventured this way.

The building erupted like an aberration, sticking out against the modest houses and empty blocks of land.

High concrete walls. No windows. Electrified fences. I couldn't help thinking that it would appear more at home in Orwell's *1984* than in this calm, inoffensive lane.

The Ministry of Untruth. The Ministry of NoLove.

Kham slowed slightly but didn't stop the bike.

"What's that?" I shouted to him.

He shook his head. I wasn't sure if he didn't know or didn't want to know or didn't want to say.

We found our way back to the main road.

Kham pulled over at a street stall.

I was no longer in the mood, so we drank beer and argued. "What's the point?" I asked. "We can't be who we are. We'll never have what we want."

"Isn't it enough? We met each other. We're here."

"We can't even tell anyone."

"We can. They understand. Anna will understand. Plenty of couples do the same. The police turn blind eye unless someone want to use against us."

"And if someone wants to use it against us?"

"Just come. We talk to Anna."

"You go. I'm tired."

Kham leaned down and kissed me on the cheek. His eyes looked sad and tired. "Call me. I pick you up if you change your mind."

"I'll see you tomorrow."

Kham walked to his bike. He glanced back, his hair falling over one eye, and smiled, before putting on his helmet and disappearing into the night.

06 November 2009

Kham wasn't there in the morning, so I took a tuk-tuk to the office. The mornings were cool now, and I shivered a little as the tuk-tuk drove down the dirt road to our office.

I knew something was wrong as soon as I walked in. Everyone was agitated, pacing, not at their desks. Anna and Kham were absent.

"What's going on?"

Ket, one of my coworkers, walked to me, visibly upset. "Kham missing."

"What do you mean?"

"We think someone take him. Last night."

I gripped the desk. "I don't understand."

Ket led me to the lounge in the common area. "We went for drink. We decide go to other place. Me and Anna in car. Kham behind on bike. We pass checkpoint, through traffic light. They stop Kham only. We turn around, go back, but he already gone. His bike still there."

"But...why? Why take him?"

Ket looked at me. It was obvious. "Anna go to police station. Still there. Talk to them. Try to find out."

Anna came back an hour later.

"I got it," she said. "I got the CCTV footage. They took him. Someone in a van took him."

"So, what do we do now?" I asked.

Anna looked at me, and I could see the resignation in her eyes. "We try."

03 December 2009.

Kham's 30th birthday. Anna and I went to the Australian Embassy again. They said, once again, that all they could do is put out another media release calling on the government to investigate Kham's disappearance. The American Embassy did the same, as did several other embassies. The CCTV footage was sent to the international media. Human rights groups demanded answers. The government remained silent.

Fear crept into the office. Hiding itself between shutters. Circling with ceiling fans.

31 December 2009.

New Years Eve. Anna invited me to her house, but I didn't go. I'd be waiting for a ghost who would never arrive.

I got drunk with strangers on beer and whiskey. I found myself at a nightclub. I hate fucking nightclubs, but I wanted to escape. I wanted to run.

Trashed enough to not care if I landed in a third-world prison, I asked around for drugs. I wanted opium. I wanted to sleep. Someone pointed me towards a youngish Thai guy. I followed him back to a guesthouse. He only had *yabba*, the little pink meth pills, so we smoked it together on a piece of foil. He looked like Kham—until I really looked and realized there was no substance to him. He was all shadow.

The shadow-Kham kissed me, and for a moment I let him. I felt everything and nothing. I paid him and I ran. I ran all the way home and locked the door. Inside, the walls seemed too small. I stalked the room like a cat in a cage.

Morning came and I didn't know if I slept or half-slept or just imagined I slept. Coming down felt shit. I didn't want to return to the world. I had nothing to smoke with, so I ate the *yabba* pill still in my pocket.

1 January 2010.

I walked the streets of Vientiane. My life disappeared behind me. Some drunk Lao teenagers invited me to drink at a street stall. They barely spoke English and my Lao was shit, which was convenient because I was no longer interested in real conversations.

I drank beer with them until I finally crashed, finding the sleep I was seeking.

4 January 2010.

Anna shook me. "Liv. Wake up."

I tried to figure out how she got in. The receptionist, maybe.

"Liv. You didn't come to work."

"I want to sleep." I pretended my eyes were closed.

"Liv. Come on. You have to get up."

"No."

She shook her head. "You don't have the right."

I turned to her.

Her face was a mix of sadness and anger.

"What do you mean?"

"You don't have the right to waste your life like this. I know it hurts. I worked with Kham for eight years. He was like my brother."

"I live my life the way I feel. Who said it had anything to do with Kham?"

Anna sighed. "Kham's gone because he wanted to make people's lives better. He wanted to make the world better. You destroying yourself is not making the world better."

I closed my eyes, and he appeared. Standing at the airport, holding a sign. On his motorbike, his hair flicking towards my face. Waking up in the bitter cold of the mountains, his skin against mine, and knowing I'd never be warmer.

And I cried for the first time. The tears I'd avoided—because shedding them meant he wasn't coming back.

"Sleep, now," Anna said, putting her hand on my head. "I'll come and get you tomorrow."

11 January 2010.

Anna drove me outside the city. We arrived at the temple on the banks of the river. We bought fish and birds to release. To make Merit.

We sat down on the cool stone steps that lead to the river.

Anna spoke without looking at me. "There was more, wasn't there? With Kham?"

"Did he tell you?"

"No. But I'm not blind. We all saw it."

I looked at the river. "I loved him." I turned to Anna. "I never told him that."

Anna took my hand. "Come on. Let them go."

I stood up and tipped the bucket. The fish plopped into the river, carrying with them all of them things I'd been afraid to say. I watched them swim away.

Anna released the small birds from their cage. "Are you okay?"

"No. Are you?"

"No." She stared at the birds disappearing in the distance. "Come on. Let's go."

We left the temple and drove to a little restaurant on the banks of the Nam Ngum river.

"I'm moving the office over to Thailand," Anna told me over lunch. "Thailand isn't much better, but the writing's on the wall here. We'll try to keep working from there. And pressuring them about Kham, of course. We won't forget him. I want answers."

I didn't reply. I looked at the water: deceivingly calm and gentle, its strong current not apparent. Keeping its secrets.

"Will you come with us?" Anna asked.

I shook my head. "I don't know how to explain. I'm not the same as I was when I came here. Something's broken."

Anna nodded. "What will you do?"

"I don't know. Maybe travel for a while. Head north. I have some savings. I'll make it up as I go along." I took a sip of my beer. The ice had already melted into it. "Do you believe in reincarnation?"

Anna shrugged. "Sometimes. My dad raised me a Buddhist. But these days, I don't know what believe, most of the time."

"I think he'd be a bird," I said. "Flying up there, away from the earth, away from all the shit and pain down here."

Anna smiled, but her eyes were sad.

2 February 2010.

I'd made my way up to Luang Prabang—slowly this time, stopping off along the way. I thought of going to Kham's village. I'd met his mum when she came to the capital, looking for answers after his disappearance, but I didn't know what I'd say to her. So, I continued further north, checking into a quiet guesthouse on a river surrounded by limestone mountains.

Just before dusk, I wandered along the bank. I sat down in a deserted spot, accompanied only by dry reeds and river plants, and pulled out the joint I'd bought from a tuk-tuk driver in Luang Prabang.

The light fell quickly. I was the only person in the entire word.

I'd almost finished the joint when I saw him.

He walked along the bank, his back to me. A cigarette dangled in his left hand, almost brushing the reeds.

Pausing in the half-light, he turned to look at me. His hair fell over one eye.

He didn't wave goodbye.

Turning back, he continued on his way, evaporating slowly into the dusk—until there was nothing but the burning end of his cigarette, which might have been a firefly, or the light of a distant boat on the river. And then it disappeared too.

A Dream
Beyond
Sorrow

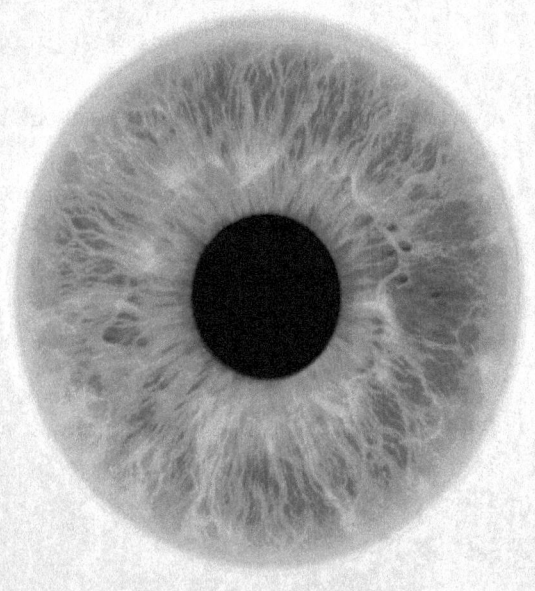

SEBASTIAN VICE

Christmas, 1992

Dear Momma,

Don't worry about me, I'm doing fine on my own. I was in a bad way a few months ago, but Hollywood will cast me one day. Some nice folks put me in a commercial for an L.A. bakery. It wasn't life-changing, but they gave me enough coin to pay rent, and I got to eat more than peanut butter sandwiches (at least for a week).

I'd say to tell Pops that I said hello, but we both know how that would work out. It's probably best if you say nothing. Although, knowing him, he'll find out regardless.

Please don't feel guilty about how things turned out. You tried to stop him from tossing me out. Pops is who he is. It took me until last week to realize that. Even the Hollywood producer I met said, "Money, fame, and wealth don't change people. It reveals them." He said, "If you make it big, kid, let me ask: Will you be a Marcus Aurelius or a Nero?"

I shrugged, knowing nothing of either man.

He slipped me a card that read, *Our life is what our thoughts make it – Marcus Aurelius*.

"What does that mean?" I asked.

The producer indulged me and replied, "Take it this way: A Buddhist monk once said something similar, and when pressed to explain more, he smiled and walked away."

It got me thinking all the rest of the night, admittedly around a growing pile of Pabst Blue Ribbon with a male friend I made on set. Sitting on the milk crate I now call a couch, long after my friend was snoring over the record collection he brought over, I realized that I revealed Pops to himself. He is what he is, it is what it is, and his nature is different from mine. Plants take in sunlight, tigers hunt for sport, and Pops hates faggots.

What is love if not completely embracing someone for who they are? Totally. Utterly. Completely. Right? The man is my father, and my love for him remains constant regardless of reciprocation. If thoughts make our lives, I want mine to be of love, not resentment.

Sure, I get that's not the way for plenty of folks. When people see me, they don't see themselves in different skin. They don't see someone who bleeds like them. They see a pale shadow of what I am: a guy who sucks dicks and takes it up the ass (please excuse the crude language, even if Pops is who I learned it from).

See, I can't blame Pops for only seeing it that way too.

Still, some part of me is compelled to write these letters. A yearly update like we discussed when you wished me well before my bus ride to L.A.. I mean, you still care, somewhere, deep inside, right? Christmas was always special to me. Remember when you bought me a Nintendo NES? Remember playing *Zelda* with me? Sure, Pops looked at me a little sideways with the care I took to organize the pink-red garland on the tree or ice the ruffles on the gingerbread cookies, but those were good times, Momma. Real good times.

Let's think of these letters like a ritual. A Christmas tradition. With youth on my side, the only path forward is up. I'll be sure to write to you each year.

Anyway, merry Christmas. Wish Mary and John a merry Christmas for me too. I don't want them thinking their older brother forgot about them.

Love,

The Unwanted Son

Christmas, 1993

Dear Momma,

What a year it's been. A place hired me busing tables (so cliché for a budding actor, I know). I'm doing okay though. Sometimes, a famous actress comes in and the waitresses give me a cut of the big tip or let me keep the autographed napkin. Obviously, I don't read much into the kiss-blot the starlet leaves on some diner tissue, but I keep it pinned to my wall as sort of a reminder that I can be the one doling out small fortunes as crumbs one day. Someone with a presence people remember, cherish.

Anyway, I did snag a few more commercial gigs! Tried out for a few films (didn't get the parts), but at least I tried. Eventually, they'll HAVE to cast me, right? Even if I'm typecast as "the gay best friend," I can put my spin on it and they can't say no forever. Right?

I've still got that actor friend I listen to albums with between auditions. I'm managing to keep in the holiday spirit even if I can't come home and he's overplaying the festive Mariah Carey hits. Oh, I met a guy, but I won't be caroling with him either. Didn't work out. Met another one. Also didn't work out. At least they accepted me. Well, they accepted me more than others. Maybe that's enough. Maybe that's as good as it'll get. Someone told me that the key to happiness is low expectations.

Anyway, merry Christmas. Wish Mary and John a Merry Christmas too. Maybe someday I'll see you all again and we can laugh about my "crazy time in Hollywood trying to cut in on the B-list" over some spiced eggnog. Pops can at least toast to my perseverance, perhaps. Here's hoping.

Love,

The Unwanted Son

Christmas, 1994

Dear Momma,

There's so much I want to tell you, but I don't have the will. My brain is foggy, and my memory fragmented. I'll do my best.

I started playing poker with some guys from the diner. My music friend was over, too, and he started playing

Nirvana. Of course, I'd heard *of* the band, but not their actual tracks. They sure sound different from Pops' Elvis records. They seemed as cool and inventive, especially this song called "Been A Son." Anyway, as the tunes blared, I brushed off the "faggot" remarks liberally thrown around during card trash talk. Things went south with my "buddies" when they asked about my sexual history.

I ended up in the E.R. with a compound fracture in my left arm, broken ribs, and a concussion. My audiophile friend tried to defend me, but I can't say I blame him for running once the broken bottles came out. Still, he was the only one who showed up as I got bandaged like a mummy. He even brought me reading material, this rock magazine where Kurt Cobain said he "could be bisexual" in another life or at least "gay in spirit" with all his disdain for mainstream macho men. The article even included a picture of all the band members performing in floral dresses. That's when my friend told me the song I liked so much, underneath all the growling guitars and sarcastic yowling, was about a father thinking of his effeminate son more like a daughter who should've been aborted. He didn't say as much, but I think my friend's sympathetic frown meant more. That maybe the dress up game we play as actors or whatever experimentation came before isn't so unusual.

I thought that was inspiring for a minute—until I remembered how the frontman met his end and why that might've been.

No more faith was garnered when my friend dragged me to the police, who just laughed off my assault as a probable "lover's quarrel." The way my friend, in too-tight leathers and two earrings that the sergeant kept eyeing, gripped my elbow didn't exactly dispel this rumor.

Reminds me of a street mural I saw on Sunset Strip: ***Police only care about property.***

Plus, I had the staggering medical bill to tend to. I tried paying the bill. Key word: TRIED.

Keeping up with those payments on top of what my landlord says I owe with how busted up the guys left my apartment and the parking lot… Let's just say I'm between homes right now.

It's not just my body and pocketbook that's reeling. A series of small cuts turned into gashes that turned into festering wounds on my soul. If you can't tell by that poeticism, I'm more than a little drunk right now. The opiates from the hospital got me feeling a little too good, got me back to my old ways. I shot heroin again the other night—not as good as the first time, but fuck it, I need something to numb me.

The first time was like your Christmas embrace. The second time, like a shadow of your love. Now, it contorts me into something resembling human. When I'm not vomiting away what scraps I steal off rich bitches' plates at the diner, I can at least feign peace-minded with a tourniquet noosing my arm.

Remember that producer I mentioned who gave me that Marcus Aurelius card? Well, turns out his thoughts haven't remained pure either. Hear he's in prison for embezzlement and got more than one or two rumors of grooming tacked to his name. Guess he became a Nero.

I found out who that was through my music friend, asking about metal lyrics, and I guess it turns out all the heroes do themselves in.

Is this what life is? A series of convulsive disappointments? Do I not even get a taste of the good life before mine descends further? I'm not asking for greenbacks or gold-plated mansions, just somebody to really have my back and call home.

I don't want to die. Not deep, deep down.

I guess I just don't know how to live.

Anyway, merry Christmas.

Love,

Your Unwanted Son

Christmas, 1995

Dear Momma,

I spent last year denying who I was. Excuse the vulgarity, but I fucked a woman to feel normal. That's the only way I can say it. Not made love to, because that's not what a "real man" is one to do. Then another girl. And another. Maybe if I practice being heterosexual, I can be. That was kinda what those diner guys were getting at before they started their sneering over my playing cards.

Maybe I can fuck my way to normalcy. "Maybe pussy is an acquired taste," my music friend laughed when I told him my plan (excuse the pun—though it did remind me of hairy lasagna). No luck so far, but I didn't initially like whiskey and now I can't get enough of it.

When I turn straight, maybe then I'll return home and Pops can love me again. Maybe I am just confused like he said. I sure do find plenty in this city and life confounding. For instance—and I shoulda seen this coming—my music friend... Well, he's not my friend anymore. Not since I started scagging again. He says he doesn't wanna see me circle the drain like I'm "method acting for *Spinal Tap*." Guess he considers cold-shouldering me a mainlined dose of tough love. Like I haven't had enough of that in my life. . .

Merry fucking Christmas.

Love,

Your Unwanted Son

Christmas, 1996

Dear Momma,

A woman vomited pity into my soul the other night and took my strung-out ass to rehab. She was an understudy for some soap opera, too sweet to laugh at my half-hearted advances after I got kicked off set. I stayed in the Fabuloso-and-failure-reeking facility for two hours before I snuck out, shot up with some bridge-dwellers, and guess what. She saw me on her commute home and dragged me back! If only I'd overdosed, I could make a Nikki Sixx joke like my album-fiend friend used to.

It may not seem like much, but I'd been clean for almost three months at that point. I told the girl as much and she said I hide lies behind my eyes, then tried to pity fuck me, use her body as some bargaining chip to rehabilitate me. When I couldn't get it up, she asked if I was really a fag. I didn't answer, but she knew. She reached for the Bible she kept in her center console. I fled the car like it was on fire.

Later that night, I met a gorgeous man who whistled at me from a café chair as I stumbled down the sidewalk. He radiated beauty, offered me a drink at the high-top, and we exchanged numbers. For a moment, he returned me to myself. For the first time in years, I didn't feel alone. I called. He didn't answer, never called me back.

A week later, the papers showed his face. He overdosed on bellinis and pain pills. I guess he endured too much existence, too. People say there's a lesson learned from everything. What's the lesson in this? That consciousness is a cruel bitch? That life consists of winners and losers, and the Lotto ball results are drawn at birth?

What has this world taught me? Life's cruelest joke is meeting the right person at the wrong time. Life's second cruelest joke is contorting yourself to fit in with people who'll never accept you—façade or otherwise. A clown regardless of makeup. Is this what that beautiful man realized? Did this fact seep into his soul such that no amount of alcohol or opioids could deaden the hollowness inside?

I glimpsed what life could be, and it was stolen away. I want my illusions back.

Merry Christmas.

Love,

Your Unwanted Son

Christmas, 1998

Dear Momma,

What more is there to say? Life repeats on a Möbius strip, the Fibonacci eating itself in an infinite swirl, and shit keeps getting worse. The books I steal from the library (can't afford a card or late fees) tell me that, but I've seen it with my own eyes. Things you couldn't imagine. Cops ramming batons up men's assholes. Bums tweaked off PCP or "wet cigarettes," clawing at each other like chickens in a cockfight until one of them is just a naked, hemorrhaging dust clump. A woman died in my arms last week. She said she had AIDS. We'd known each other for weeks, but she never spoke her name.

Daily, I bear witness to someone shot in the head, or stabbed, or raped, or any number of horrific things. As for me? I stopped auditioning. What's the point? I'm clean and back busing tables at another diner (away from the poker bros). Maybe this is as good as it gets. Maybe life is just a freak show of humiliation and degradation. I tried fucking my way straight again. Maybe I'm God's puppet with the strings cut. Doesn't seem like pussy will cure me. Smoking space rock and watching the life leave friends' eyes couldn't move me to change, so, fuck it.

This is goodbye. I don't think I have much time left anyway. Sorry for all these letters bringing bad news around Christmastime. Shouldn't have been spreading my depression around like disease, like a dirty needle. Listen, I want you to stay chipper for Mary and John's sake. May they never feel a tenth as lowdown as I do. They're normal, got a lot going for them, so I won't let my negative energy taint their chances at a happy life by writing you folks or phoning around when it's way too dark to think straight anymore. For what it's worth, I always knew you loved me, but never felt it's full force.

I just comprehended it in the cold way one knows 2 + 2= 4.

I'm sorry—deeply, that I couldn't be what you and Pops wanted. What I fooled myself into thinking I could be. No more cowering. Gotta face my fate, but I'll do it "Softly," not leave too much of a mess, like that old Elvis song Pops used to play. I leave, giving the last bit of love I know wasn't wrong to you guys, my family.

Love,

Your Unwanted Son

Christmas, 2002

Dear Momma,

If you're reading this, you probably found it on my corpse, or maybe a cop gave it to you. Maybe I mailed it (I don't know. I took a lot of pills like that beautiful man in the papers). Doesn't matter, since, to state the obvious, I'm dead.

Is this a suicide note? A confession? An explanation of the end? Call it what you will, these are my last words.

There's so much to say in these final moments but I can't choke out the words. Maybe some things are better left unsaid. Maybe you don't deserve to see the shivering child hidden within. I decided to return for Christmas, to see you all again, to see if I was good enough for Pops. As I looked in the window, I saw you, Pops, Mary, and John. I saw Pops carve the Christmas turkey while you all laughed. Wearing eggnog mustaches, nibbling on gingerbread men. Surrounded by garland so red and sparkly, it burned my eyes. No music was playing, but as I turned away, Elvis's blue crooning filled my ears.

You didn't need me. I guess you could call that "window pain." What am I now but a stranger to you? As I walked away, I realized I'm a stranger in my own skin. My body is foreign, as if the flesh isn't mine, but nobody else's either. I don't know when it happened, but my mind is divorced from my body. I wager it happened when my homosexuality became an invitation to rape.

I won't get into all that, though it might've been the tipping point in seeing all the small violations in my life tally up into a brutality too great to ignore. To massive to want to trudge along with the weight cutting into my shoulders.

Maybe my biggest mistake was seeing people for what I wanted them to be, not as they are. Maybe life's cruelest joke is cursing me to see the world the way it should be. I heard that while listening to Tupac with my friend-turned-stranger, if memory serves.

So, this is it, Momma. This is where my story ends. Last year, I learned the word *aphorism*. It's a small, ironic truth. Relapsing a few times and pinballing in and out of rehab left too much time to think. Let these pithy words, presented in no coherent order, define the finality of my life.

You can be anything you want except yourself.
Life is what happens between dissociations.
Years passed, and more and more of myself slipped away until a stranger looked back in the mirror.

All I wanted was a shoulder to cry on. Someone to share my pain. Someone to see the world through my eyes.

I've spent too much time looking outward because I couldn't find the will to look inward.

Fate condemned me to death before conception.

What has all this led to? After all these years, and an ocean of tears, what can I display but "window pain"?

Before the pills do me in, right at the last nanosecond, maybe I'll realize what this whole cosmic shitshow is about. I'm told that happens. Guess I'll find out.

Dying a fraud is the American way.

Poverty isn't a problem. The humiliation is.

We're all slaves. The impoverished are bound with rusted chains. The rich with gold ones. As for those in the middle? They get fucked at both ends. Existence binds them with chains of HOPE and FEAR. They beg for gold chains, and tremble at the thought of rusted ones.

A buddha is tethered by no chains.

To avoid overdose, reality must be ingested in microdoses.

The experience of people and the experience of pain is the same.

Showing respect is an invitation to disrespect.

Helping people is like helping snakes. Both are lethal.

A gaslight is brighter than the sun and grows cancer of the soul.

The harder you try to unfuck yourself, the more fucked you become.
The line is thin between humility and self-loathing.
There's a place beyond sadness. Beyond depression. That place is eternal resignation.
Life is gambling. Most quit while behind.
Enlightenment isn't a lofty or elevated state of being. It's the place you descend after falling into a place beyond Hell.

Momma, I can't say I love you anymore. Such words were automatic, but, in my final moments, I refuse to deny what I feel. My smile vanished so long ago, all that remains are snow-crusted tears.

Regards,

The Unwanted Son

Christmas, 2005

My Beloved Son Mark,

I hope this letter finds you well. I haven't heard from you since things turned sour. Last month, you turned 30, and I have a surprise for you. Time softens a man, and your father has come around. Last year, he almost died in an accident on the mill, and that was a wakeup call for him. You said you'd write me, but I never got your letters, and all of mine were returned, unread. I tried many such addresses I thought you'd be at—called around any casting agencies and low-income tenement buildings I could get a hold of—but no luck.

I do hope you're hanging on and harboring no grudge, though I'd understand it, darling.

Gosh, I still remember you putting on little plays for my girlfriends and me after our soaps ended. Even then, everybody said you had a great little spark they could see on stage one day. I hope you found your way and maybe a little fame even if I'm too far away to glimpse it. It's certainly deserved after all the impromptu drama we put you through.

Anyway, onto greener pastures, you'll be happy to know John finally started playing drums a few years back. (Instead of just saying he was gonna be a big rock star like Elvis with no work behind it.) It all sounds like noise to me, but he says his band is close to signing with a major label. Heck, maybe he can score one of the films you're in one day. As for Mary, she is finishing up college. When she tells me about biochemistry, it's over my head. She's undecided if she wants to be a pharmacist or do graduate work and become a research chemist. Whatever it is, I hope she can help people. Seems too many young folk are in a bad way these days.

Gosh, all these years passed, and there's so much I want to tell you. I hope you return home soon, or at least write to me. Your father wants to apologize, and I just want us to be a family again. I miss our little tradition of rolling out the dough for Christmas cookies and trimming the tree. My eyes get all misty every time your father spins "I'll Be Home For

Christmas" on the record player or I hear John break out a *Zelda* video game with the silly little MIDI soundtrack.

I'll keep writing you, Mark. Know I love you, and please know I have too many regrets to count. We weren't perfect parents, but we tried. Are trying. If I never hear from you, I pray that, somewhere, out in the vast world, you find a dream beyond sorrow.

Know we send all our love if only a little too late,

Mom

OXOX

More
from
Anxiety
and
Outcast
Press
Charity
Anthologies

THE
PLACE
WHERE
EVERYONE'S NAME IS
FEAR
WITH AN INTRODUCTION BY
MONICA DRAKE
AN ANXIETY/OUTCAST
PRESS ANTHOLOGY

STORIES THAT STAB LIKE A KNIFE

AN ANXIETY-INDUCING, NOT-ELEMENT PRESS ANTHOLOGY

MIRRORS
REFLECTING
SHADOWS

A/O